IQ
ROOM TEMPERATURE

A Novel by

ROBERT GOTTLIEB

IQ Room Temperature
First Edition

Previously published in 2012 as No Nude Swimming, A Lawyer's Way Out, and substantial portions of this book appeared in Courage to Grow Up, published in 2021.

ISBN: 979-8-9868010-0-1 (ebook)
979-8-9868010-1-8 (Paperback)

The identity of some of the authors of quotations and comedic monologue used in the book could not be ascertained by a reasonable search. As authors are identified, recognition will be given appropriately.

Printed in the United States of America

To Steven Garber (1947-2012),
my friend of forty-seven years,
who bravely and indomitably fought an
illness that ultimately took his life.
And to Mary Beth Garber,
Steve's wife of nearly forty-one years,
who made every sacrifice of dedication
and support a person could ever
consider or undertake.
I miss Steve's friendship, honesty, humor,
and perspective on life.

To Thelma Gottlieb (1924-2011),
my mother, who fought death until she had
no more strength to battle for her survival.
My mother survived the German Blitz
over London in World War II. After WWII
she enjoyed her life devoted to her husband
and children in the San Fernando Valley.
I miss picking up the telephone
to hear her voice.

IQ Room Temperature

The Charles Manson Trial began in the Los Angeles County Criminal Court House in July, 1970. The prosecutor for the Los Angeles County District Attorney's Office was Attorney Vincent Bugliosi. As I recall, in a televised news conference outside of the courtroom, a news reporter's question to Mr. Bugliosi was, whether Mr. Bugliosi believed that Charles Manson was guilty of Sharon Tate-La Bianca murders? Vincent Bugliosi's answer was, "Anyone with the IQ of room temperature would know Charles Manson is guilty."

Acknowledgements

This book has come to fruition thanks to the contributions of a number of people.

I am grateful to Chiwah Carol Slater for her skilled rewrite and edit of the book and for her inspired collaboration in helping me carry my voice into the story of *IQ Room Temperature*.

It is my good fortune to have enjoyed extraordinary friendships, some for many decades. I appreciate my friends' generosity and caring for my best interests. From laughs and fun to advice, my friends have given the support that allowed me the focus to write *IQ Room Temperature*. Special thanks to Lynne Alana Delaney and Ruben Gomez, Stan Wertlieb, Sid Franklin, and Ray La Tulipe, R.I.P.

1

Pain is inevitable.
Suffering is optional.
—*Haruki Murakami*

Had I looked, I might have seen the first punch coming. But I never had a clue about the knockout.

The sun was just beginning to warm the house on that cool, clear Sunday morning in late spring as I sat in my kitchen reflecting on my good fortune.

Gazing out through the broad glass doors, beyond the manicured lawn and glistening swimming pool to the beauty of San Diego's Mission Bay, I was one with the limitless ocean that stretched away to the pale horizon.

A spectacular 180-degree view. It cost a bundle, but my law practice paid for it. Life was good.

My wife's striking reflection appeared in the glass as she came from behind to stand between me and the view. Turning to face me, she looked beautiful as ever.

Her long blonde hair was pulled back to show off her magnificent bone structure. The quality cut of her pale blue silk blouse accentuated the sleek lines of her body.

I smiled.

She did not. “I am getting a divorce,” she announced.

Her words bounced off me. “From anyone I know?” I quipped, setting my coffee down on the table.

She sighed. “Sam, why do you always do that?”

“Do what?”

“The wise-guy answers. You’re always making a joke. You don’t take me seriously.”

Intent on maintaining the peace and contentment I’d felt just before she released her thermonuclear device, I shifted my gaze to take in the blue of the ocean and the two or three fluffy white clouds hovering above the horizon.

“I take you very seriously, Cindy,” I said, reconnecting with the steel of her eyes. “But I can’t believe you’re serious about this. You want a divorce? Why?”

“Oh, I am serious. I want a divorce. Now. And I just told you why.”

The note of finality in her voice cut right through me. “But how are you going to live?” I objected, still reeling from the blow. “I mean, before you met me you shopped at Target. Now you shop at Nieman Marcus and Sax 5th Avenue.”

I regretted the words as soon as they left my tongue.

“I want you out of the house,” she said. She turned and walked away, heels clicking on the hardwood floor.

That was the first punch.

My head spun. She wanted me to move out? It wasn’t going to be as simple as that. Nothing was going to be simple.

We had three children, after all. What about them? How would they feel about seeing their dad kicked out of his own house?

I sat there for a few minutes, struggling to get my bearings. Finally I got up and crept upstairs to the bedroom, where I knew I'd find her.

Sure enough, there she sat, leaning toward the mirror over her hand-carved mahogany dressing table, fixing a smudge in her eye makeup.

"Cindy, can we talk about this?" I ventured.

"There's nothing to talk about. I've made my decision."

"But—what about the kids?"

"They stay with me, of course."

"Look, Cindy …" I sat down on the foot of the bed, looking at her image in the mirror. "I love my kids! And they love me. You can't just break up our family like this," I pleaded. "It's not right. No matter how you feel about me, you have to consider the kids."

Anchoring her hands on the edge of the dressing table, she turned slowly in her chair and looked straight at me, her eyes cold as polar ice. "Samuel, I am thinking of them," she said.

Ach, Samuel. I hated it when she called me that.

"No, you're not," I countered. "You're only thinking of yourself."

"Hah! How would you know who I'm thinking of? According to you, I don't think at all."

She had a point there. Very little that she did had ever made sense to me. In the beginning I'd been so stunned by her beauty that it hadn't mattered.

It hadn't really mattered later, either. I had learned to live with it. I didn't expect her to make sense.

She turned back to the mirror and resumed playing with her makeup. "I repeat: I want you out, now."

"So … we're going to share the kids?"

She didn't answer, and I plowed ahead. "You can't stop me from seeing my kids, you know."

She shrugged. "No problem. I know how attached they are to you. You can see them as often as you like. I'm the one you can't see. I'd be just as happy if I never saw you again."

What could I say to that? I turned to go back downstairs to make sense of this encounter with Cindy. We had never been a stellar fit.

She liked caviar; I preferred chips and dip. She liked five-star hotels; I preferred rustic bed and breakfasts. How had we managed to build a life together?

From the first, she had enjoyed the benefits that came with having a lawyer for a boyfriend. And I had been awed to find that a woman with her matchless looks would be interested in me.

Finally, after three years of dating, she had wanted more. "When is the big day?" she had asked.

"Every day is a big day," I'd countered. Sarcasm was an old habit, my first line of defense when I didn't know what to say. That time, it made her laugh.

Three months later, I woke up married. Fourteen years ago … or was it fifteen? I counted. Fifteen.

Looking back, I saw that the last half of our marriage had been edgy. Nearly adversarial at times. There had been clues.

But I had been too wrapped up in my career to pay attention.

The realization that she wanted me out had knocked the wind out of my sails. But, being a practical sort, I took a deep breath and regrouped. I was going to have to find a new place to live.

I went out to my car to get my cell phone and grabbed a property management firm's business card I had stuck in the visor.

Rather than go back into the house, where I obviously wasn't wanted, I gave them a call. They had an apartment they thought I'd like.

I turned the key in the ignition and set off to have a look.

2

If you don't understand it,
I can't explain it.

—Robert Shrum,
Democratic Strategist

The sun blazed so hot I could feel it burning my back and neck as I sat in an aging deck chair at the edge of an apartment swimming pool, doing my best to read every line of a lease agreement.

It was hard to see through the emotion. This was only a one-year lease, but twenty-five years as a litigation lawyer dictated that I read every word.

Amelia Lopez, the leasing agent, stood in front of my chair, staring. "Mr. Weisman, are you all right?"

She was a petite, dark-haired Spanish woman with just a barely detectable accent that showed up more in the cadence of her speech than in the actual words.

"Yes, I'm fine, Amelia," I said. I wasn't, but I didn't like wearing my feelings on my sleeve. "I've just had a surprise, that's all, and I'm not sure what to make of it."

"Oh?"

"Yeah. Usually, an employee is terminated at the end of

the day on Friday, or on Monday morning when they come to work."

Amelia frowned. "Excuse me?"

"Today is Sunday," I explained. "So I can't decide whether I was terminated, or exterminated."

Her eyes widened. "Have you lost your job?" she asked.

I laughed to put her at ease. A light breeze flapped the green and white umbrella on the round metal deck table as she sat down in the chair next to me.

"No," I said, realizing she must be wondering how I was going to pay the rent. "I don't have a job. I have a law firm."

Her face relaxed. "Oh, good. Well, I think you will like this complex. There is a vacancy on the second floor with a view of the pool," she said. "Exactly what you asked for."

She was probably in her late thirties, I judged, with a pleasant face and a nice figure. I couldn't help admiring her long black hair, the way it reflected the sunlight.

An apartment complex certainly was not where I'd expected to be at this stage in my life, but it would do for now. "I'll take it," I said.

"Good, good!" Her smile was warm. It brightened her whole face and made her big eyes glow.

Doing my best to appear sharp and lawyerly, I picked up the agreement and thumbed through it.

"Everything looks pretty standard as apartment leases go," I said, "but I do have a question about the Lease Addendum." I pointed to the page. "It's about these three words."

She pursed her lips. "Our lawyer put that in there to protect us. Everything is about liability these days. No one cares about responsibility anymore."

"My concern is, I have young children, and I don't really want them to see anything of this nature when they come to visit."

"You're married?" Her eyebrows shot up in surprise. "I mean, it's nice to see a concerned parent."

I gave an offhand wave of the hand, as if I were speaking about a client whose problems had nothing to do with my life. "She asked me to move out."

"Oh, I'm sorry."

My mouth was dry and my stomach hurt. Oh well. This was no time to be focusing on that. "So tell me about the Lease Addendum," I said.

She drew in a breath and pointed across the pool, beyond a group of young men and bikini-clad girls I took for college students, and two gray-haired men, all busy batting a large ball back and forth in the pool.

Caught up in my own preoccupation, I hadn't even noticed their laughter and conversation. Now I noted that they seemed to be having a lot of fun.

I couldn't remember the last time I'd had fun. And not just in my marriage. It had been a long time since I'd laughed in my career, too.

"Mr. Weisman?" Amelia was calling me back from my thoughts. "Over there, on the far wall?"

A large white sign with red letters on the other side of the pool bore the three words I was concerned about in the Lease

Addendum: 'NO NUDE SWIMMING.'

I felt my lips twist in something between a smile and a frown. "So … nude swimming is a problem here?"

She leaned toward me with a serious expression on her face and spoke as if in confidence.

"On weekends, the college students go clubbing downtown until past two in the morning, then come to the pool to swim and hang out after drinking and partying. They used to go into the pool, and even the Jacuzzi, in the nude."

She hesitated briefly and leaned closer. "And they would have sex."

Despite the concern I'd expressed about my kids, my first thought was that I should have moved here sooner.

"Isn't that why parents send their children away to college?" I asked. "So they don't do it at home?"

"The college students were only part of the problem," she said, keeping her voice low. "Our real concern is with the older residents in their late sixties and seventies, our senior citizens."

"Ah," I nodded knowingly. "The seniors were offended."

"Not really," she replied. "Senior citizens don't often need eight hours of sleep. Or sometimes they go to bed so early that they wake up at four in the morning. Some of the hardier ones would go to the pool, or the spa. They would swim in the nude, too. And," she said, leaning closer again, "they would also have sex."

She looked at the pool for a moment, then back at me. "One of the older men had sex with a college coed and suffered a heart attack. It was a mess. The gentleman was okay, but the owners were terrified. If it happened again and one of the seniors died, the apartment complex could be sued as a contributing factor in a wrongful death claim."

"I see," I said, still wondering what it might be like to swim in the nude with college girls.

My cell phone rang. I didn't recognize the number. "Hello?"

"Hi, Sam. This is Alfonso Lechuga." I had no idea who Alfonso Lechuga was. "I know your father from the plastics business," he explained. "Your dad told me about that guy you defended, the ultralight airplane manufacturer."

"McBairn. Yeah, so?"

"How you dug and dug until you found the evidence that showed how they'd set him up."

"Yeah, he was framed. Very savvy scheme, but they missed one little detail."

"And you found it."

"Okay. So what about it?" I didn't know what this guy was after, but I knew I didn't have time for it now.

"You saved his business. He was going down, and you didn't let it happen. That took guts, and determination. Very impressive."

"And? So what's that to you?"

"Your dad told me to call you about a legal problem I have."

"I'm sorry," I said. "Who are you again?"

"Alfonso Lechuga. Your dad said I should call you. He told

me you would do a friend a favor."

I couldn't keep the irritation out of my voice. "It's Sunday, Mr. Lechuga. Please call my office next week."

I put the cell phone in my pocket. "I keep telling him not to do that."

Amelia looked confused. "Telling who not to do what?"

"My dad has people call me for legal help," I said. "Then he tells them I'll handle their problem for free. It makes my father look like a great guy to his friends. But it takes up my time, and I lose money. Of course, like a schmuck, I always do the work."

"At no charge?"

I nodded, frowning. "At no charge."

"I think it's very generous of you to help people who are less fortunate," she said.

"You don't understand," I snapped. "These people can easily afford my fees. They're cheap, and they don't want to pay for my services. If I asked them to do something for free, they would say no. They would want to get paid full price for what they do."

Amelia's cell phone beeped. "Yes?" She listened, then said, "Tell him to come down to the pool." To me she said, "There's someone at the office for you. They sent him down."

A well-built man in his thirties, wearing dark slacks and a gray polo shirt, strode directly up to me at the table. I'd never seen him before.

"Are you Sam Weisman?" His voice was low and forceful, his eyes sharp.

"Yes," I said, getting to my feet. "Who are you?"

He shoved some papers at me. "You've been served."

I glanced at them and turned to Amelia. "My divorce papers." I paused. "We were married for fifteen years. And we celebrated six of them. The rest? For the kids, I guess."

I shook my head in resignation. "And now this."

She said nothing.

"You know," I went on, "what's hers is hers; what's mine is negotiable."

Amelia's eyebrows went up, but she didn't say a word.

Realizing that the process server had not moved, I frowned at him. "Anything else?"

"Yep. I have another one." He whipped out a second set of papers. "You've been served again."

I read the first page. My knees didn't turn to jelly. And I didn't collapsed back into the chair. I managed myself from pushing him into the pool.

"How did you even find me?" "We have our ways." Turning away, he walked briskly to the front gate.

"What's the matter?" Amelia asked with concern as I flipped through the second set of papers.

"My partner. He's suing me for dissolution of the law firm," I said. "He's alleging that, per our partnership agreement, we split the debt and he retains all the assets and the clients."

"Oh, no," Amelia sympathized.

"Well, it's Sunday. Nothing bad can come of this in the next twenty-four hours."

John Lennon's voice blasted out "*Money –That's What I Want*"- on the cell phone in my pocket. *The best things in life are free- But you can keep them for the birds and bees- Now give me money that's what I want*

"It's my father," I told her, grabbing the phone. "He has this thing about that Beatles song, so I set his calls to *Money-that's what I want.*"

Opening the phone, I held up my hand for her to wait a second. "Yes, Dad."

"What's the matter with you, Sam?" His usual frontal direct attack. "She's a gorgeous girl, best thing that ever came your way. What happened?"

"I don't know what happened."

"What do you mean, you don't know? Why didn't you listen to me?"

"I did listen to you. I gave her the big house, the pool, the Mercedes. Look, this was not my idea. She's the one divorcing me."

"You're crazy," he said. "I'll call her, see if I can straighten this out."

I tried to slow him down. "I'm taking care of everything," I said. "I found an apartment with a view of the pool. And, yes, I'll talk to the kids. Haven't had a chance yet. They weren't home."

I listened for another minute with the phone held away from my ear. "Okay, Dad. I'll talk to you later." I put the phone back in my pocket.

Amelia still looked sympathetic, but her voice held a hint

of disapproval. "I'm sorry for eavesdropping, but does your father always tell you how to live your life?"

"He doesn't tell me how to live," I retorted. "As a matter of fact, I've gotten some of the best advice ever from him. You wouldn't believe the experiences he's had."

Amelia said nothing.

I sighed. "At least he hasn't found out about my partner suing me. He thinks I'm still on the ropes, but that was the knockout punch."

I shifted in my chair, puzzling over my predicament. Things hadn't felt right in the office the last few weeks, I realized. I'd been feeling a peculiar distance with James and his staff, but nothing I could put my finger on.

My cell phone started singing in my pocket: *The best things in life are free- But you can keep them for the birds and bees- Now give me money (that's what I want)!*

3

When in danger, when in doubt,
Run in circles, scream and shout
—*Herman Wouk*

Driving to the office, I felt surprisingly good for a Monday morning. The car's climate control maintained the exact temperature I liked.

I pulled into the parking lot, turned off the motor, and sat staring for a moment in the warm silence.

It was a classy looking southern California rancho style office—two stories, white stucco, with a red tile roof and black wrought iron stairwell, shaded by overhanging palm trees and surrounded by giant orange and blue Bird of Paradise plants. Just seeing it reassured me.

My marriage might be over, but I still had my work, my clients, my career. Surely the lawsuit threat had just been my partner blowing off steam.

He was the excitable type. A misunderstanding, a surge of emotion between partners. Definitely not a knockout. I had overreacted.

Now that I'd been served, though, I thought about some of the terrible situations I had seen break up some attorney and business partnerships.

No, James couldn't be serious about this. I had given him everything he'd wanted. This was just a bump in the road, a wrinkle that would be easily ironed out.

After all, we were people who argued, screamed, and shouted for a living.

I grabbed my leather briefcase from the back seat, straightened my tie, locked the car, and walked briskly up to the stairs.

I would get through it fine. We'd had our ups and downs before, my partner and I, but I had been a litigator and trial lawyer for a long time. I was used to setbacks.

I hopped up the stairs, practically whistling. Pushing through the glass doors, I headed past the front desk.

My partner's office door was closed. Must have an early client meeting. I shrugged, opened the door to my office and walked in.

I stopped cold.

Other than my custom-made, specially contoured, back protecting, lumbar supporting, kidney massaging therapeutic desk chair, there was not a piece of furniture or a client file in sight.

No desk. No file cabinets. No couch. No client chairs. No lamps. No plants. No pictures. Nothing.

"Beware the furniture movers," I heard myself quote from the movie Head Office. One of my favorite movie lines.

I dropped my briefcase on the floor and dropped like a stone into my chair.

I stared into the blue space out the window, where the

tops of the palm trees shivered in a slight breeze. This had gone too far.

Flipping open my cell phone, I dialed the police and explained the situation. "My partner has served me and locked me out. He had my furniture moved out," I said, keeping my voice as level as I could.

"Has he committed any act of physical violence in the last thirty days?" the detective asked.

"No, no, but this is my office. He's just a partner I brought in. He can't do this to me."

"I'm sorry, Mr. Weisman. There is nothing we can do. This is a civil matter, not all that different from a divorce, and unless there has been physical abuse we have no jurisdiction. We cannot get involved in a feud between two attorneys. I'm sure you can understand."

I didn't understand, but nothing I said would sway him. I closed the phone.

"What are you doing here?"

I spun around in the chair. James Watkins, my partner, stood in the doorway, arms folded over his polo shirt.

Tall and good-looking in a sporty, country club sort of way, he embodied the essence of what I like to call "the other three S's": Shallow, Self-Absorbed and Stupid. (Fitting stand-ins in for the standard "Shit, Shower and Shave.") His posture was relaxed but his expression was firm.

"It's my office," I said.

"Not any more. We're not partners any more, Sam. Go home."

"James, we need to ..."

He held up a hand to stop me. "You know I can't talk to you, Sam. We're adversaries in a lawsuit. Someone will be in touch with you."

He turned and walked away.

"But James, you can't..." I was too dumbfounded to put a sentence together. "The furniture. Where...?"

I heard his office door close.

Silence, except for the echoing sound of a printer running and phones ringing down the hall.

I stood up and looked around at my office, until this moment the office of a highly successful lawyer. Now all I could see were the deep creases left in the carpet when the movers took the sofa and the credenza and bookshelves out.

My next thought was that his mother had raised a moron. I was going to prove it but didn't know how and when.

He had the jump on me. The element of surprise. But he wasn't going to get away with this. Who the hell did he think he was?

"I brought you into this law firm, James," I said softly, addressing the bare wall. "I started this firm. I did all the hard work before I ever thought of bringing you in."

I turned and stormed out into the hallway. My throat was so dry I could hardly breathe. I felt the blood pounding in my neck.

At the water cooler, I grabbed a cup and drank two glasses, one after the other, gazing around, struggling to get my bearings.

Suzi Moreno, the paralegal, was at her desk, busily thumbing through briefcase law. She glanced up at me over her black-rimmed glasses.

"Suzi—" I started.

"I can't talk to you, Sam. I'm prohibited." Her attention went back to the book, ignoring me.

Funny. When I'd hired her, years earlier, she'd thought I was the greatest attorney in the United States. Maybe the greatest in the Western hemisphere.

Now I was invisible. This would not do.

I walked down the hall to James's office, threw the door open and charged in.

"Get out," he ordered, his eyes cold and mean as he rose from his desk and came at me. "Leave now, Sam, or Annalee will call security."

"James, this is my f*%!ing lawfirm!" I yelled. "You can't take it away from me! Where did you get such a crazy idea?"

"No, Sam, it isn't your law firm. It's *my* law firm. It hasn't been yours in a long time. Partners, remember? Well, I've terminated the partnership. By the terms of our agreement—which you signed, if you recall—upon termination, it became *my* law firm.

I couldn't believe what I was hearing. "That's crazy. You're a nut case, James. What the hell are you talking about?"

James frowned. "Sam, you agreed to all the terms and conditions. You signed the agreement. It sounds like you didn't even read it." His voice was even, measured. Patronizing.

"Of course I read it. I'm an attorney!" I fumed. "I know

what it says! Get it out, and I'll show you!"

"Where's your copy?" he countered.

"In the office file." I turned to go get it.

"Hold on, Sam," he said. "It's right here." He held it out to me.

I reached for it and opened it to page three. "There," I said, pointing to the relevant paragraph.

"Oh? Read it to me."

I read: "'In the event this partnership is unilaterally terminated, all debts shall be evenly divided between the two parties to this agreement, and all assets and all clients and cases preexisting this Partnership Agreement shall remain the property of the terminating partner.' What?!"

Livid, I turned to the final page. My signature at the bottom hit me square between the eyes.

James shook his head. "Get out, Sam. And get yourself a lawyer. You're going to need it."

Realizing that my fury put me at a disadvantage, I took a deep breath.

"I am a lawyer, James," I said softly. "And the last thing I need right now is advice from a scoundrel. I don't know how you did it, but you… "

I turned on my heel and strode toward the main door. On the way I passed Annalee, James's gorgeous assistant. She glanced up at me with a slow shake of her head.

I nodded and walked on by, aware in spite of myself of the delicate scent of her perfume. It had affected me so profoundly that I had bought it for my wife for Christmas.

I couldn't think about that now.

At the front desk, Patty was transferring a call to James's office. Wearing her headset, she managed to look cute and businesslike at the same time.

I made my best attempt at a smile. "Hi, Patty."

A look of sadness came over her. "Oh, Sam…" she said, her voice tremulous with compassion. "I'm so sorry. I can't talk to you because of—you know."

"You're in on this?" I shook my head in disbelief.

"You were always so nice to me, Sam," she said softly. "You remembered to ask about my mother's condition. You brought me flowers—and not just on Secretary's Day. I just want you to know… well… thank you, but…."

"Oh, screw it, Patty," I said.

The office phone rang, and Patty hit the button. "James Watkins Law Firm," she intoned.

I couldn't stand it. Turning to leave, I stopped short. Two things struck me: first, that I'd forgotten my briefcase, and second, that my name had already been razored off the front door. It read: THE WATKINS LAW FIRM, not WEISMAN AND WATKINS LAW OFFICE.

Stomping back into my office—or what had been my office—I grabbed up my briefcase from the floor, next to the chair.

My chair.

Hesitating for only the briefest instant, I threw my case into the seat and rolled the chair forcefully out of the office, down the hall toward the front doors.

"Mr. Weisman!" Patty protested. "I don't think…"

I ignored her and burst through the doors and out onto the landing. Bang! Bang! Bang! Down the metal stairs I went, all the way to the sidewalk and parking lot below, shoving the chair with every ounce of determination I had. The wheels roared across the asphalt.

"Sam! Sam! Stop!" James shouted from the balcony. I kept going, undeterred.

"Hey!" I heard him pounding down the stairs. I pushed harder. His shoes slapped on the pavement as he ran across the parking lot behind me.

"Sam, hey!" He caught up and stood in front of me, forcing me to stop.

"What?" I demanded.

"What are you doing?"

"It's my chair!" I said. "And I'm taking it with me." I felt like a dog with a ball in its mouth. I would not let go.

"It's not your chair."

"Are you kidding? It cost me nearly four thousand dollars, James! I love this chair. I paid for it. It's mine."

"The firm paid for it," he said. "It's our asset. You know that." He took hold of the opposite side of the chair and pulled. I yanked back. The chair mamboed between us, back and forth.

"Give it to me!"

"I won't. Get your hands off it!"

He let go of the chair and lunged at me headlong, butting his head hard into my chest. I reeled, inadvertently pulling the chair out from under him, dropping him flat on his face on the cement. He didn't have a chance to put his arms out to break the fall.

"Oh, f-me!" he groaned, bringing his right hand up to cover his nose and lip as he rolled onto his back, his knees in the air now.

Somehow I had managed to keep my feet. Too angry to care that he might have broken his nose, I wheeled the chair to my car.

I had left the top down. Well, at least something was going right. I tossed my briefcase into the passenger seat, then picked up the chair and laid it on its back in the back seat.

Hoping James wouldn't recover and be hot on my heels, I jumped over the door into the driver's seat and turned the key in the ignition.

A glance over my shoulder told me that Annalee and Suzi were rushing to his aid. Great. Now I had become the villain.

I shot out of the parking space and sped past them before I caught myself and slowed down on my way to the exit.

My mind whirred. What the hell was going on? Had that clause been in the agreement when I signed it? No, it couldn't have been.

Though I couldn't recall reading the agreement before signing it, of course I had. And it had been drawn up by Allen Martin, an old-time lawyer my father had used before I passed the bar.

Martin would never have put in anything unfavorable to me. I missed that old guy. He had passed away a few months earlier.

My stomach hurt. I realized I was breathing fast and shallow, and my heart raced.

The sound of squealing tires, rending metal, and busting glass came from the boulevard in front of the law office. Two cars were stopped at the intersection, one plowed into the other.

Clouds of steam poured out of the car behind. The driver of the front car staggered out, one hand holding his neck and the other gripping his lower back.

Quickly, with a glance back to make sure James wasn't coming after the chair, I stopped and got out of my car and walked through the palm trees lining the street.

When I reached the man, I took out a business card and wrote "witness" on the back and handed it to him.

"You've got a great case," I told him. "Call me if you want me to handle it for you."

I knew I shouldn't have said that. It wasn't kosher. Too late. It was done. And it gave me an odd sense of satisfaction.

The guy looked at me, his face contorted in pain. He looked pale and weak. "Right now, just get me some help," he said.

I forgot about James. "Here," I told him. "Have a seat." I helped him over to the low block wall in the shade of the palm trees.

Whipping out my phone, I called 911 and gave them a description of the accident and explicit directions to the scene.

Closing the phone, I told him, "They'll be here in a few minutes. Don't worry." He nodded, glassy-eyed, still rubbing his neck.

Walking back to my car, I glanced up at the office. My office. It had always been mine, and it would be again.

"Take that, Watkins," I said with a smile, flashing my fingers in a Victory "V" up toward his office window, where he would have gone to lick his wounds.

Why had James decided he needed to get rid of me? Was it just greed? Or was it his way of trying to prove himself to himself?

I had taken him on in a moment of weakness. I'd been producing enough work for three attorneys, and had a regular flow of case files to offer an attorney who would relieve me of my multitude of responsibilities.

A mutual friend had told me about James, touting him as an experienced trial lawyer, the rainmaker at the firm he was with. We had set up a partnership.

James had brought no case files with him, but that hadn't struck me as a problem, since I had an overload. I was the rainmaker. In the two years he was with me I gave him files valued at more than a hundred thousand dollars.

But James had turned out to be a disappointment as a partner. Although he was a competent attorney, his surly and demanding disposition made him unpleasant to work with most of the time.

I had toyed with the thought of terminating him as a partner. Hah! I should have. It doesn't pay to be Mr. Nice.

My cell phone rang as I was opening my car door. I pulled it out of my briefcase. "Sam Weisman," I answered in my lawyer voice. It might be someone calling with a legal problem.

"Hello, Sam. It's Alfonso Lechuga! Your dad said to call you? I tried your office, but they told me you no longer worked there."

"Ahh—I'm in the middle of something right now, Alfonso," I said as I turned the key in the ignition. "Call me back later." He was still talking when I closed the phone and dropped it onto the seat.

All I could think was: Why had I ever gone into law?

Yet Alfonso's call came as a reminder that I was an excellent attorney. What was it he had said? Guts and determination. Yes, and a quick mind. I worked hard to protect my clients. I made sure they got the best deal.

Still, uncertainty gnawed at me. Could I really have been so stupid as to sign an agreement that gave away my clients and all the firm's assets? I tried to recall looking over our agreement. Had it been a client's case, I knew I would recall every word. But my own? Maybe I'd gotten sloppy.

My immediate next thought and concern was that if I continued emotionally out of control, my actions going forward would not be smart enough to rise to the level of intelligence to be stupid. And if not smart enough to be stupid, I would with certainty lose my contest with James to recover my law business. My first step to becoming smart was not to do something stupid and rise above the IQ of room temperature.

This discussion with my brain helped relieve my distress. In the short passage of time after my confrontation with James, the burden of becoming smart escaped my consciousness.

4

The dogs bark,
but the caravan moves on
—*Arabic Proverb*

There's something tranquil about bodies of water. Even a pond or a swimming pool can have a profound calming effect.

I sat on a cloth-covered chaise lounge on the warm pool deck at the apartment complex, soaking up the sun and suntan lotion.

A gentle breeze cooled my chest, blowing across skin speckled with droplets of water where my kids had splashed me a moment earlier.

"Rachel!" I called out to my oldest. "Make sure the boys have enough sunblock on, especially Ryan. He burns easily."

"Yes, Dad," she replied with that theatrical gesture of boredom thirteen-year-old girls major in.

Rachel was a beautiful blonde like her mother, but with so much more composure in the face of life's ups and downs. Off-the-scale bright, she had character and fortitude to go with her intellect and class.

The boys were my hellions, especially Ryan, the youngest.

He thrived on being the baby.

Adam, the second child, was our rebel. Like a lawyer, he would invariably answer a question with a question. Cindy insisted it was because I was a lawyer; she said it had rubbed off on Adam. I thought he was just trying to define himself by rejecting me.

Adam was almost twelve, but he had started rebelling at age three.

At the moment he was lying on a towel about twenty feet from me, wearing dark sunglasses and black trunks. The trunks went well with his deep tan and good looks, he'd told us, not to mention his James Dean mysterious facial expressions.

How he knew anything about James Dean was beyond me.

I watched Rachel chase Ryan around the pool with her tube of sunblock. He let her get close, then giggled and splashed her before bounding away.

Ever the dutiful, responsible sister, Rachel followed after him.

"Hi, Mr. Weisman!"

I turned to see Amelia Lopez walk past with a prosperous looking couple and what appeared to be their college age daughter, a slender, striking girl with a black pageboy haircut.

I waved to Amelia. I wanted to say hello, but she had already gone on with her tour, touting the features of the apartment complex to her new client.

Ryan let out a screech from the pool. I straightened up

from the chaise lounge to see him covering his face with his hand while Rachel stood by the edge of the water with her hands on her hips.

"Rachel," I called out, "what's going on?"

"She hit me!" sobbed Ryan.

"No, I didn't." Rachel rolled her eyes.

"She rubbed that cream in my face on purpose!" Ryan blubbered. "It stings! I'm going blind!"

"Ryan," I told him, "settle down and get out of the water."

He climbed out of the pool, dripping on the hot concrete.

"Come here," I said. I stood and wrapped my arm around him. "Now take your hand away so I can see."

His eye looked fine. "There's nothing in your eye. It's on your face. Here, put the sunblock on yourself. Then you can go swimming again."

He took the tube and stomped off, glaring at Rachel.

"What happened?" I asked Rachel.

She leaned toward me. "Nothing. He just likes to complain and make a lot of noise."

"Okay," I told her with a half laugh. "Enjoy the pool."

She beamed, and then turned to Adam with a twinkle. "Hey Jake, when Ryan's done, you need to put some more on too."

"Yes, Sarge," he groaned, and then turned over to lie on his stomach, ignoring her.

She looked back to me. I gestured for her not to worry about it and took my seat again.

Pulling my sunglasses down over my eyes, I lay back to

simmer in the warm, moisture-inducing sunlight. I caught a bare hint of salt on the offshore breeze.

I tried hard not to think about my soon-to-be ex-wife, my office, my father, or my house. It all threatened to shatter my peace of mind.

Behind me someone said, "You've got beautiful children, Mr. Weisman." The slight Spanish accent told me Amelia had come back.

"Thank you." I smiled at her. "Have you met their father?"

She smiled.

"Sometimes, they really push my buttons."

"Oh," she laughed, "they are young. That is their job." She squatted down right next to my chair, almost kneeling. "You are very good with them. Firm, but not too demanding."

"Well," I said, "with three of them you get used to the noise. They can hit a hundred decibels in a heartbeat."

Her face took on a serious expression. "They know you love them. And they know you are the boss. You should be proud."

I looked away for a moment. Rachel was watching me with Amelia, but I knew she couldn't hear our conversation. The other two were far enough away as well.

"I made myself a promise," I told Amelia solemnly, "I wasn't going to do to my kids what my father did to us. I've gone to great lengths to be involved in their daily lives and show affection."

"That's very nice to hear." Amelia reached up to tuck her dark hair behind one ear with a lovely feminine gesture. Then she looked past me, and her face changed.

"I'm back, Sam."

The voice of the woman who seemed to want me to sing in soprano came from behind my lounge chair. I could feel her plan to destroy me: Cindy had returned to pick up the kids. She looked nice in her tennis whites, short skirt and hair tied back.

"Cindy," I said, "this is Amelia Lopez, my leasing agent. She found me the apartment." I started to explain to Amelia, but she had already risen to her feet and was brushing the wrinkles out of her skirt.

"Pleased to meet you, Mrs. Weisman," she said formally, and then turned to me. "You have my business card, Mr. Weisman. Let me know if you need anything." With a glance at Cindy, she walked off toward the front gate of the complex.

Cindy tilted her head at me, her voice dripping with implication. "Sam, put your ego back behind your zipper, where it belongs."

"Kids!" I stood up. "Your mother's here. Time to go."

Adam did a slow rollover and sat up. "We just got here," he muttered. "What's the rush?"

I bit my tongue to keep from saying, "Ask your mother."

Rachel was trying to round up Ryan, who had splashed away from her at the other end of the pool.

"Sam," Cindy said, "I'm having trouble paying for the yard maintenance, the pool, the Jacuzzi, the utilities and everything. It's just too much."

"I make the mortgage payments," I said, making an effort

to control my temper, "plus both car payments, the insurance, and all your miscellaneous bills."

She sailed right on. "I've found a house for me and the children, but I'm going to need part of your proceeds from the sale of our house to pay off my debts so I can qualify for the mortgage."

She lowered her chin a bit, looking up at me with a forlorn twist of her lips. "It's for the children."

"I'll think about it," I said, honestly considering that they would need a good place to live.

Rachel came up with Ryan in tow, wrapped in a towel and squawking at his sister about something. He grinned at Cindy. "Hi, Mom!"

Adam sauntered over and stood in dark silence for a moment. "Beware the furniture movers," he said.

"That's not funny, Jake," I said, scowling at him.

"It's what you always say," he answered with a shrug.

Cindy just smiled.

I turned to Rachel. "You have everything? Towels? Sunblock? Flipflops?"

"Yes, Dad," she said. She puckered her lips and gave me a kiss.

"Love you, kids," I told them.

We said our goodbyes and Rachel herded the boys toward the front gate. I couldn't help but admire her initiative.

Cindy walked after them. Over her shoulder she shot back at me, "I meant what I said about the proceeds from the house, Sam."

I practically bit my tongue in two, determined not to argue in front of the kids again. Then the wrought iron gate banged shut behind them, and they were gone.

It was not yet noon and the pool area was empty. A rich, endless blue sky arched overhead.

My patience had been stretched to a tiny thread, and I lay back down on the chaise lounge in the sunny warmth and tried desperately to find that elusive sense of peace I had felt earlier.

"At least I have a pool," I said softly to no one in particular. Out here there were no irritating phones ringing with people asking for free legal advice, no adversarial confrontations, no lists of demands.

Well, Cindy had a demand, I reminded myself. But all in all, it was quite pleasant. I could feel my muscles growing less tense. My eyes closed in peaceful repose.

Yap! My eyes flew open. Yap! Yap! I sat up. Yap! Yap! Yap! I stood up and looked around. Yap! Yap! Yap! Yap!

Right above me on the apartment balcony overlooking the pool stood Mrs. Larson's tiny Yorkshire terrier, fiercely determined to state its territorial claim. Apparently I was in its view.

"Be quiet. No barking, please," I asked nicely.

Not only did the yapping not stop, it grew faster and louder. This was ridiculous. What was wrong with this dog? Was it a battery operated barking machine?

I wanted to march up to Mrs. Larson's door and demand she take the dog inside, or maybe I could complain to the manager's office.

But she had paid the pet surcharge, and the complex rules allowed animals on balconies until ten. I had found that out when I'd complained the first time.

Yap! Yap! The dog challenged me with a tiny growl. I closed my eyes, feeling the red cloud of rage rising. "Shut up!" I said. "Stop barking!"

Yap! Yap! the dog answered me, and growled louder.

"Stop barking!" I repeated. "Stop it! Stop it! Stop it!"

The dog continued to bark, even faster. My commands fell on deaf ears. The dog was really getting on my nerves.

"I told you to stop barking!" I was shouting by now. "This is the last time!"

For just a brief moment, the dog cocked its head and looked at me. I thought maybe I had gotten through.

Then it started barking again. This time, it didn't stop.

"What's wrong with you?" I yelled. "Don't you understand English?" Whoa! I caught myself. My emotions had swung out of control. Of course the dog didn't understand English. It was, after all, a dog.

A young string bikini-clad coed with a towel wrapped around her waist walked into the pool area at that moment.

It was the slender, black-haired girl from before, the one with the family Amelia had been showing through the complex. She was startlingly attractive, pale and imperious.

"Don't use people psychology on a dog," she said, her tone powerful and self-possessed. "Use dog psychology. Be a pack leader."

She glanced up at the dog. "Don't you watch *Dog Whisperer* on the History Channel? Cesar Millan is the man, the dog man. Don't yell at the dog. Do the 'Shush!' It shocks the dog's brain and makes it submissive."

She looked right at me with a gaze that felt like a cold laser. "I use it on my boyfriend all the time, " she confided, smiling with a wicked gleam in her eye, sizing me up. "He does whatever I tell him to do. Boyfriends, dogs, they're all the same."

She sashayed on past me, letting the towel fall away to reveal a delightful southern exposure.

I didn't say anything. All I could do was mumble to myself, "Yes, ma'am. I'd like a burger to go with that shake."

The girl looked up at the dog as she passed under its balcony. "Love you, pup," she said to the dog, her voice a silky purr. "Shush, boy, shush! Be a good boy. Do what I say. Lie down. Don't move. Stay."

The dog grew quiet and lay down with his head on his paws. Total submission. With just a hint of triumph, she glanced at me and walked away toward a chaise lounge set near the Jacuzzi.

"Money (That's What I Want)" Startled from my daydream, I grabbed my phone off my towel.

"Hi, Dad."

"Sam, I talked to Cindy about this mess."

"Don't talk to her!" I said. "I'm taking care of it."

"Hey, I got the whole story," he blazed on. "You're a nitwit. You don't treat her right. I tried to tell you, but you've got a bowling ball for a head. She's a girl. You gotta be a gentleman with her. But no, not you. You talk to her like a railroad worker. You give her orders. You never listen to her."

"Dad, I don't do that…"

"I'm telling you to give the girl a break, Sam."

"She's breaking me!" I stammered. "I'm spending a huge amount of money—covering my bills, and all of her bills!"

"And why haven't you called Alfonso back?" my father went on. "He has a real estate deal for you."

That was it. "For what?" I bellowed into the phone. "A space in some apartment building in National City? I'm tired of you sending me deadbeats! I can't afford to work for free for your friends and customers. I went to law school so I could get paid for giving legal advice. You're asking me to give away my time, Dad. My time is my life!"

The dog was up and barking again with ear-piercing intensity.

"But, Sam…"

"There are no 'buts'!" I was practically screaming. "Stop sending these people to me for free legal services!"

The dog was barking with such violence that it bounced around stiff-legged on the balcony, each yap producing a short hop. It looked like a bunny having an epileptic seizure. Yap! Yap! Yap!

"Just think over what I said," he said.

"I'll talk to you later." I closed the phone. I could hardly catch my breath. My face was red, and I could feel the veins pulsing in my neck.

The dog continued to bark, its yap even more shrill than before. It would not quit. I thought about calling the dark angel to work her spell again. But instead, I gathered up my belongings and trudged back to my apartment.

Yap! Yap! Yap! Yap! Yap!

5

> Learning is something you
> need to be emotionally
> ready to receive.
> —*Bill Lucas, author*

I swear, every time I walked into my apartment it seemed to get smaller, all jammed together like I was back living in my old college studio.

"I do not belong here!" I shouted out loud. "This is not my life."

That made me feel better. But now I was acting like Ryan.

Running my hands through my hair, I lay back against the rental sofa and wondered what I was going to do with myself.

I had calmed down a bit. Yet though I no longer wanted to break up the furniture, the sense of loss still stung.

I had to get out of here. If I sat around and stewed in my own juices, I would leave a puddle of stomach acid burning a hole through the sofa, the floor, and down into the apartment below.

Where would I go if I went out? I hadn't the faintest idea. I never went out, especially alone.

That thought gave me an idea. I grabbed my wallet and

thumbed through the business cards. Why not? What did I have to lose?

I pulled out the card, grabbed my cell phone, flipped the lid open and dialed. It rang once. I snapped the phone shut. I hadn't asked a woman for a date in nearly twenty years.

"But you're a lawyer," my inner voice chided. "You deal with conflict and confrontation every day! Get over it! It's just another cold call."

"Call her, you nitwit!" my portable parent chimed in. In this case, my father was right. I punched in her number again.

"MesoAmerican Leasing. This is Amelia Lopez," she answered in her business voice. Her soft Spanish accent played nicely on my ears.

"Hi," I said. "It's Sam, Sam Weisman."

"Oh." she sounded taken aback.

"Is this a bad time…?"

"It's okay," she said quickly. "How can I help you, Mr. Weisman?"

I plunged ahead. "Honestly, Amelia, I'm going out of my mind in this little room."

"Oh." she sounded disappointed. "You are unhappy with the apartment?"

"No, no," I stammered.

"I can find you another apartment."

"No, Amelia, that's not it." I tried to sound reassuring. "I just, well, I'm going out to dinner tonight and I don't really want to eat alone."

A long pause, then, "Are you asking me to have dinner

with you? Is this a date?"

"Well," I laughed, "actually, yes. I'm not used to being alone, and I don't want to sit in a restaurant by myself, surrounded by strangers. How would you like to come and keep me company?"

"Let me see…" her voice took on a playful lilt. "Yes… yes, I believe I am free this evening."

And just that quick, I was on top of the world. I assured her I would make all the arrangements.

We met at Freshwater Frank's, my favorite seafood place, down on the water.

Amelia looked magnificent, her black hair glowing with a freshly-washed sheen. And she was charmed by Frank's rustic atmosphere, with its weathered boards and creaky window flaps.

The place looks like a drunken sailor's dive, its walls covered with old life preservers from 1930s merchant marine vessels, bills of lading, pieces of wooden crates with exotic destinations like Tonga and Mozambique stenciled across them.

The food was out of this world. It didn't matter that Frank had never been on a boat in his life, not even a rowboat. He knew how to prepare seafood.

As we ate buttered scallops and dipped our shrimp in Frank's special seafood sauce, Amelia wiped her mouth and met my eyes. "Tell me, Sam…" she started, hesitating.

"Tell you what, Amelia?" I smiled to encourage her to continue, doing my best to ignore the people at the table behind me. They were talking about, of all things, a court case.

I found myself listening in spite of myself. I had to restrain myself from turning around to give legal advice.

Amelia touched her tongue to her lip. "Your father has not called once the entire time we have been together this evening," she said.

"I turned off my phone," I said. "Every time I'm with you, he calls. I think he must sense I'm out having fun, so he's got to do something about it."

She looked baffled. "What?"

"Never mind." I waved my hand in a dismissive gesture.

She went back to eating with a slight shake of her head.

The noise in the restaurant had increased. Not only the talking, but the terrible clatter of dishes and silverware being cleared and the rattle of ice being poured into pitchers.

"You have a very interesting relationship with your father," Amelia said.

That raised my eyebrows. "'Interesting' is an interesting description," I said. "Actually, he is quite an inventive businessman. In addition to his tailoring business, which he's always done, he's also been successful in plastics recycling and real estate."

I picked up a shrimp and dipped it. "In fact, he may have been the reason behind many of the real estate laws we have today." I chomped the shrimp in two and chewed.

Amelia laughed. "What do you mean?"

"My father is a networking genius," I said. "He pretty much single-handedly invented modern California real estate syndications. Other people might have done it before him, or elsewhere in the country, but no one I know of was nearly as successful or forward-thinking."

"What did he do?" She seemed genuinely interested.

"It all started back in the fifties, when he wanted a backyard pool. To him, a swimming pool symbolized the California dream, the good life, freedom, wealth, success.

"He was a men's custom tailor with a growing family," I went on. "He didn't have the cash for a pool. Only wealthy people and country clubs had swimming pools.

"The banker wouldn't qualify him for a loan because he didn't have the income. His tailoring business was doing well enough, but the house and his family demanded all that he earned.

"He had survived the Great Depression and World War II. As you may be aware, his was the 'can-do' generation. Men like my father were dreamers who whetted their fantasies on the impossible.

"He didn't see obstacles; he saw opportunities. He desperately wanted that pool, but he didn't have enough in his pockets. So, he had to figure out a way to use the money from someone else's pockets."

She was fascinated now, hanging on every word, gazing directly into my eyes as I told her my dad's story.

"He devised a plan to finance the pool by others sharing the cost of construction. He told everyone of his customers about the pool, and asked them if they were interested."

"If they paid into his fund, he wrote their name on a cardboard spool—you know, the kind they wrap bulk fabrics around."

She nodded.

"He started raising money with the contributions of about two hundred customers, business relationships, and all their friends and families.

"In exchange for their investment, he gave his promise that they could swim in his pool anytime they wanted. And, most importantly, they could bring their friends and families."

"Really!" She was hooked on my story.

"Yeah. The pool ended up not costing him a cent. And it made him new friends and customers like crazy. Everybody who came to swim knew somebody, and each of them brought somebody else."

"It gave him an endless stream of new customers—more neighbors, more of their friends, strangers my father never knew, and more of every kind of person imaginable—all delivered right to our patio. Our pool became a networking center for people who would have never met otherwise.

"Fascinating," she said.

"Yes. And nationality didn't matter. Race didn't matter. Everybody's money was good."

Amelia laughed.

"Dad's pool syndication plan was a great success. That's how he became really well-to-do, by applying the pool syndication plan to real estate deals. As a real estate speculator, my father was way ahead of his time."

"That is an extraordinary story," Amelia said, wide-eyed.

I smiled. "And the banker who denied my father a loan

to build the pool? He ended up swimming at our house. He became a big investor."

I could tell Amelia was impressed. Her eyes shone bright in the soft candlelight of Freshwater Frank's.

The voices behind me had grown louder. The guy was telling his wife, or his date, or whoever it was, that he had saved on lawyer's fees by representing himself in court. The only reason he'd lost the case, he said, was because the judge wouldn't listen to him.

I leaned over to Amelia, indicating our neighbors with a move of my head. "Of course he lost the case," I said. "You know what they say about people who try to be their own lawyer? 'Anyone who represents himself in court has a fool for a client and an ass for a lawyer.'"

Her lips curved into the tiniest of smiles as she went back to the subject of fathers. "My father has never left the land where we grew up," she said. "It belonged to his father, and to his father before him."

Her smile broadened and a hint of mischief lit up her eyes. "So… my father owns real estate, too, in Catemaco, Veracruz."

Real estate in Mexico? Maybe there was more to this woman than I had anticipated. Apartments? Commercial buildings? "What sort of real estate?" I asked.

"He is a farmer."

Immediately the image came to my mind of Amelia in some small, dirt-poor rural Mexican setting. I saw chubby children with food-smeared faces wearing worn-out clothes, and skinny dogs running around.

She must be really lucky to have her job as a rental agent, I realized.

Amelia broke into my thoughts to ask, "What is your father's name?"

"Benjamin," I said. "But everyone calls him Ben."

"What should I call him?"

"Mr. Weisman," I smiled.

She nodded, not realizing it was supposed to be a joke. But then, she would probably have called him that anyway, given how well-mannered she was, not overly familiar with anyone.

She said, "My father's name is Cesar Patricio Lopez Romero."

"Wow, that's quite a name."

"We preserve the names on both the paternal and maternal sides. In Latin tradition, the custom of giving children surnames from each parent goes back to the Middle Ages."

"So why is your name Lopez if his last name is Romero?

"The father's name comes before the mother's in my family's custom. Romero was my mother's maiden name."

Just then, Frank shuffled over with our main course.

Amelia's father might have a fancy name, I thought, but he probably dressed in white farmer's garb and one of those giant straw sombreros, and walked around leading a burro like the peasants in The Magnificent Seven.

As I cut my fish, Amelia dug around in her purse. She pulled out an old wrinkled photograph of an older Mexican man with a mustache, dressed in white, wearing a sombrero and pushing a wooden wheelbarrow in front of a vegetable garden.

"Your father?" I asked, inwardly cringing. She nodded with a bright smile. Why did I always have to be right? "Nice wheelbarrow," I said. What else could I say? Although I could have commented on his hat.

She nodded with pleasure. "Yes. He's very proud of his vegetable garden."

I didn't know what to say. I just kept eating.

Amelia swallowed and pointed at the fish with her fork. "It is very good, the fish." That made me feel better.

"Today, at the pool," she began. "Your wife, she's so beautiful, and so are your children."

"Oh," I said, grabbing my napkin to wipe my mouth, "you don't know her. She can be a witch of the highest order when it comes to me."

I must have had a pained expression on my face, because Amelia reached out to put her hand on mine. "Is there something wrong?"

"As the famous Paul Harvey said, if something can go wrong, it will," I said. "You wouldn't believe what she's pulling on the sale of the house."

The guy behind me was getting louder. "The judge kept telling me to clarify myself," he said. "I did that! I told him exactly what had happened and what I had done. I didn't get my three hundred dollars' worth of value. I don't care about the money; it's the principle of the thing. If he was any kind of fair judge, he'd have given it to me!"

I leaned toward Amelia, "The judge was right," I said, louder than I meant to. "He should have lost the case."

Feeling a tap on my shoulder, I turned around to see a forty-something man in an expensive suit, a very corporate-looking guy, standing behind me.

"Hey!" he said. The voice didn't fit the man. He looked like a Gentleman's Quarterly model, but he sounded like Rocky Balboa. "What do you mean, I should have lost the case?"

I couldn't resist. "You lost the case because you don't know the process, what to say, how to say it and when to say it. You should have hired an attorney. You probably would have won."

I turned back to Amelia and told her, "He could have easily won that case if he knew what he was doing."

I wiped my mouth with the napkin and threw it on the table. "The guy," I said to her, "is the perfect example of why no one should ever represent himself in court."

All my frustrations welled up in me, begging release. I couldn't help myself. In a louder voice, to make sure Mr. Know It All Business Corporate Man heard me, I said, "You put roller skates on an ape and you think you've got a dancing partner. It's still an ape."

I turned slightly in my chair to get an angular view of him. He was squinting so hard at me I thought his face would break. "What?" he spit out. "What the hell does that mean?"

I shrugged. "It means you may have the best case on earth, but if you don't know the courtroom dance, then as far as the judge is concerned, you're more likely to lose your case."

I said it with a smile. I noticed that another man seated at a nearby table smiled with me.

The wannabe Clarence Darrow stood up and turned toward me. I stood up, too. I didn't know what to do after that.

Apparently, neither did he. We stood there face to face, a safe six feet apart, for what must have been a full minute—two guys doing a guy thing, neither having any idea where to take it from there.

The voice of reason had a message for me. "Take your own advice," it told me. "You're not a boxer. You're a fish restaurant customer. If you want a fight, hire a boxer. If not, sit down and finish your meal."

Damn! What I wanted was Sugar Ray Leonard telling me to lead with my left and follow through with a right.

Thank God for Frank, who walked over and placed himself between us to defuse the situation.

Amelia had hold of my arm. "Sam!" she said, looking distressed.

"I'm all right," I said, a bit embarrassed at this point.

Everyone went to extremes to play it down. Frank was cordial and offered to buy everyone a drink. The other couple left shortly afterward. Amelia finished her dessert. But I had lost my appetite.

When I asked Frank for the bill, he smiled. "It's on the house. But next time I need your legal help, remember to give me a credit."

Out in the parking lot, I listened to the rolling surf below. Amelia stood close to me and looked up into my eyes.

"Sam," she said gently, "you are a good man, but you are not all right. You almost got into a fight with a stranger. You are stressed out. Every little thing upsets you. You almost got beat up on our first date. You really need to see someone, someone you trust. You need to get some things off your chest."

I didn't want to admit it, but I knew she was right. Every little thing was getting to me. "To tell you the truth, Amelia, I'm shocked at my own behavior," I replied. "I've never been like this. My emotional response in there was over the top, way out of proportion to the situation. I'm afraid I'm going off the deep end."

She squeezed my hand. "No, you're not. You're under a lot of pressure, and you need to talk with someone who can help you find your balance."

"I don't know anyone," I said. "I can't unload to just anyone, and especially not to someone I don't know."

"What about your father? He knows everybody. There has to be someone you can talk to. A relative, an uncle, someone."

I thought for a minute. "Well, there is Sid the Psych."

"Who?"

"Dr. Sidney Gold." I sat up. "One of my father's investors in the pool venture is a psychiatrist. Everyone calls him 'Sid the Psych.' He loves that. I don't know why."

"Do you think he will remember you?" she asked.

"Oh, yes." I stifled a laugh. "I haven't talked to Sid in years. We could catch up on old times. He was always a kidder."

"Will you go see him?" she pressed.

"Absolutely not." I opened her car door. "I don't need a therapist. I need a life."

6

We hear what we want to hear
and disregard the rest.

—Simon and Garfunkel,
"The Boxer"

The next afternoon found me sitting in my car in the parking lot of a large, modern La Jolla medical office, looking northward at the endless miles of the blue Pacific Ocean, past the La Jolla sandstone palisades and sand beaches.

Heaving a sigh, I stepped out of the car and walked toward the front door.

"What am I doing here?" I asked myself.

I pushed open the big glass door and entered the lobby. The hot looking, well nourished, tan bodied young receptionist greeted me.

"Can I help you?"

In my mind I answered, "Absolutely!" But I was on my best behavior. "I'm here to see Dr. Sidney Gold," I said, thinking as I said it that I would much rather sit on her couch than his.

"Down the hall to the left," she said pleasantly, pointing. "On the right, Suite 150."

Moments later I stood at the door marked "Sidney Gold, Psychiatrist." I stared at the door, shook my head, and went in.

I was greeted by another good-looking young receptionist. "Welcome to Dr. Sidney Gold's office," she said. "How may I help you?"

I began to think that maybe this was not going to be as bad as I'd heard. No one I knew who had been to therapy had ever mentioned the receptionists.

All I had heard about was the weeping, the rage, and the crushing disappointment when they discovered how lousy their lives were, and especially how much they hated their fathers.

I didn't hate my father. I just wanted him to stop calling me so often.

"I have an appointment with Dr. Sid. I mean, Dr. Gold," I fumbled. "He and my father have been friends for decades." Why did I feel I needed to explain?

"Sure," she said. "Sam Weisman. We have you at eleven. You're early." She motioned to a couple of chairs and a coffee table under a giant picture window. "Take a seat. We have some fresh ground whole bean coffee and health food cookies, there on the table." She pointed. "Dr. Gold will be with you shortly."

I took a seat and gazed out over the magnificent sand beach. It was pleasant being away from my lonely apartment, sinking into the comfort of the overstuffed leather chair and enjoying the view of the Pacific.

This seemed like a good place for me—quiet and comfortable, with great coffee and tasty cookies.

The door to his Dr. Sid's office opened. "Sam!" he said, coming out to greet me. "Good to see you!"

I struggled to swallow my health food cookie, brushing crumbs first onto the floor, then into my hand, chewing with haste as I searched for an ashtray or a napkin.

"Oh, don't worry about that." Dr. Sid waved his hand. "Come on in! Good to see you. I just spoke to Ben last week." He made a facial imitation of my father. "You know, 'My son, the lawyer.'"

He laughed good-naturedly, and his whole face lit up. His good humor was infectious. I couldn't help smiling. He shook my hand and ushered me into his office.

"So, Dr. Sid, how've you been?" I managed at last. That made him smile even broader.

"Thank you for remembering, Sam."

"You've always been Dr. Sid," I said. "In my business I meet a lot of doctors, but you're the only doctor I know with his nickname monogrammed on his shirt."

"It makes a good ice breaker." His facial muscles moved in what bordered on a wink. Ushering me in, he showed me to another comfortable chair and took one himself, choosing the one beside me rather than the one behind his desk.

"As I look at it, Sam, you and I are in similar businesses," he began. "Yes, the people who come to you are called clients, while those who come to me are called patients. But in both cases, they come looking to us to solve their problems, don't they."

"That they do, Dr. Sid."

"And many times those are problems they themselves have created, and continue to create, regardless of us or what we do. Right?"

"Oh, so right," I replied with a knowing laugh.

"Well, the business we're in is about people and solving these people's problems that I call "psycho-ceramics."

"Psycho-ceramics? I don't get it. We're in the pottery business?"

"Yeah sort-of, We both deal with crackpots."

I couldn't resist a laugh. "Okay. So psycho-ceramics is dealing with crackpots."

"You got it. An inside term of the trade. That's what we do, you and I." He steepled his fingers and made eye contact. "So, what's going on? Tell me."

"I'm not sure what to say," I started, feeling my shoulders rise in a shrug. "I don't even know why I'm here."

Dr. Sid threw his head back and laughed heartily. "That's rich, Sam."

He looked at me warmly. "Of course you know why you're here. You just don't want to admit it—especially to a psychiatrist, who you're afraid will make some ominous medical pronouncement about your condition that you didn't expect. Then suddenly your whole life is in the toilet."

He looked like a comic who had just told a joke and was waiting for the audience response. It took me a moment to realize he was serious.

"Well, it's not that bad," I said. "But, sort of."

"Listen, take it easy, Sam." He held up both palms to me in a calming gesture. "Don't try to analyze anything. Just tell me what's been going on."

"Honestly..." I took a deep breath. "It feels like my whole life just blew up in my face. I'm worried about everything. My clients, the kids, what I'm going to do with myself.

"Nothing's working the way it should be. Everything's noisy, irritating. No one cooperates. Everyone ticks me off. I'm annoyed with myself and everybody else. I can't sleep."

I knew I was ranting, but I couldn't stop. It felt so good to get this off my chest.

"The phone rings and I get upset—I mean crazy upset, like I want to scream and holler and break things. I don't, of course, because that's not me. But these people keep calling... salespeople, complaining clients, people expecting legal services for free.

"My father calls and it feels like I'm having a stroke. I feel pressure in the sides of my head and down the back of my neck, and a tightness in my shoulders, like I'm ready to explode.

"I go to a restaurant, and the guy sitting behind me wants to start a fistfight. And then there's this barking dog at my apartment complex that just won't shut up. It could shatter glass with that bark."

Dr. Sid watched me with such a serene expression of compassion that I felt guilty for whining.

"I just can't handle all this," I said at last. "Can you do

something for me?"

"Of course," he said evenly.

I waited for him to say more, but he kept silent.

Finally, he smiled. "Well, Sam, you're lucky. I don't help crazy people. I help people like you. Your situation is normal. Yes, it's dysfunctional. But it's normal."

I cocked an eye at him, and he understood that I didn't really get what he was saying.

"First, there's normal and there's abnormal," he explained, "and then there's functional and dysfunctional."

He waved on hand in a gesture of dismissal. "Let's forget the abnormal; they have problems I don't want to go into. Of the normal people in our society, at least ninety-five percent and more are dysfunctional.

"I divide my normal but dysfunctional patients into two separate categories. Now, here's what you need to know: The first category of dysfunctional I call D&D, and the second I call A,D&D."

"So… what is D&D, and what is A,D&D?"

Dr. Sid's face betrayed just a suggestion of a grin, and I knew that meant he was enjoying this.

"Well, Sam," he said, "D&D is Dumb and Dangerous, but usually only to oneself. A,D&D, on the other hand, is Angry, Dumb, and Dangerous. A whole 'nother level of dysfunctional. Those folks are a menace to society."

Suddenly, it all burst out. "Well, I don't know which of those categories I fall into. I am angry, but I don't think I'm a menace to society," I said.

"However, I am under an enormous amount of stress right now. I'm in a lawsuit with my partner over the dissolution of the law firm—the one I built. We have a preliminary hearing in two weeks for division of the property, client files, my fees, and the firm's debts."

"In other words," said Dr. Sid, "you need to be emotionally stable enough to represent and defend your interests."

"Well, yes. Plus, I'm also in divorce proceedings with Cindy. She filed an Order to Show Cause for spousal support, child support, house payments, even her personal maintenance—hair, manicure, pedicure and massages at Stefano Orlandi's salon."

"Oh, yeah!" he said. "My wife goes there. She loves Stefano. She says he has great hands."

I stared at him for a moment. "Dr. Sid, she's prevented me from selling any of my assets. On the one hand, she wants to bankrupt me."

I frowned. "On the other hand, she wants me to pay for everything. Instead of psychotic, she's bi-chotic—you know, she wants it both ways. It's making me nuts. I've got to find a way to get rid of her without losing my shirt!"

"Hmm, bi-chotic," he said. "I like that." He smiled on one side of his face. "What about visitation for your kids?" he asked.

"That was odd," I said. "I told Cindy what I wanted and she gave me everything regarding custody and visitation with the children without an argument. She even signed an agreement."

Dr. Sid leaned forward. "Okay, you've been through some major losses. Your wife dumps you. You lose your law firm. It's understandable that all that is sending you into stress.

"By the way, in case you're still wondering, you're definitely D&D. Your anger is situation-based, not the core of your reality. It sounds like you need some counseling, somebody to hold up a mirror for you so you can begin to see how you get yourself into situations that smack you upside the head."

He chuckled. "Here's my first recommendation: You should go find yourself a nice girl and have a nice dinner at a nice restaurant. Relax. Take a load off."

"I just did that," I said.

He brightened. "And how was it?"

"She told me to come see you."

"Ahhhh." He sat back. "Sam, you're overwrought. You're frenetic. Your emotions are running wild. You need to relax. You're trying to control two situations that are pretty much out of your hands at this moment."

I was beginning to feel morose. "Maybe I was never suited for the practice of law."

"Oh? What makes you say that?"

"Listen to me!" I said bitterly. "Do I sound happy with my life? But then, what else am I going to do? It's all I know."

Dr. Sid sat forward again and folded his hands. "What are you doing for money?"

"I have a couple of small personal savings accounts in my name," I told him. He watched me, saying nothing.

I sighed.

"I trusted James, my partner. He wasn't much good in court, so I handled most of that and gave him administrative control of the office operations, which he was good at. Including payroll.

"And now he's stopped my paycheck. He shut down our business checking account and opened a new one I have no control over.

"As part of all that, he controls the money market account. At the end of the day, I'm lucky if I have control of my bladder!

I sat back in my chair. "There are some ongoing receivables I'm entitled to, but he's in control of those, too. My clients will want to come with me, I'm sure, but it's going to be a battle."

"Why is that?" Dr. Sid asked.

"Our signed agreement says we split the debt and he retains everything, including my clients."

Dr. Sid straightened. "Why would you sign an agreement like that?" he asked, incredulous.

"I don't know. I couldn't believe it myself. I had had James put my original into the company file, and he gave it to me when I went in the other day. I went over it, and yes, that's what it says."

I jumped up out of the chair, crossed the room, and stood looking out the window. "It's crazy. I know that wasn't in there when I signed it. I can't imagine it was. But it's there. And my signature's on it. It's insane."

I turned back to face him. "Was I out of my mind? Do people do crazy stuff like that.?"

"All the time."

"I know." I sat back down in the chair. "My clients do stupid stuff like that. And then they come to me to get them out of it."

"Well..." Dr. Sid frowned. "You've got to unlock some money. Call your clients. Tell them you are not with the law firm anymore and they can stay with you.

"Remind them how long you've been working for them, aggressively representing their interests and protecting them against financial loss. Remind them that James has never handled any of their legal matters and doesn't know any of the details of their cases."

"That might not be possible. James will try to stop it. And because of the lawsuit, I can't get at any money. I have to figure out how to get around the partnership agreement."

"What about disability insurance for your emotional condition? Are you covered?"

I hadn't thought of that. "As a matter of fact, I am." I perked up. "Thank you for mentioning it."

"I'm just considering all the possibilities and protecting my financial interest here," he said. "I'm not giving you consultation for free, you know."

Dr. Sid made it easy to talk about myself. He asked about my mother, my sister, my children, and he listened carefully.

He guided me around what he called 'deadly whirlpools of our own making.' He didn't let me get away with anything.

"Sam," he said, "your unrealistic fears are blowing everything out of proportion. And your fear is dangerous to you. People can feel it—your children, your friends, your clients—and it scares them away."

Dr. Sid stood up. I followed, assuming the session was at an end. "Sam," he said, laying a hand on my shoulder, "You're a little depressed. It's normal after what you've been through."

He leaned dramatically in my direction. "I have to ask, have you had any ideations of suicide?"

"Suicide? Never. I would never give anybody the satisfaction. Homicide, yes. And I have a short list."

He frowned, and then his face melted into a wry smile. "I appreciate your comedic humor," he said. "You're a funny guy, just like your father."

He rubbed his chin in a gesture I took to mean he was giving serious thought to the subject of our conversation.

"There's more to it than that, of course, but that's the heart of the matter. In the psychiatric biz we say you have unresolved anger and guilt, and you're questioning the sanity of your own behavior. I just like to say we're going to get you back on track."

I didn't know what to say.

Dr. Sid went on. "Now, I believe in pharmaceutical solutions only when absolutely necessary, and then only for a brief time. But medication might help you manage your emotional ups and downs during these stressful times. So in this case I'm making an exception."

"Dr. Sid, I don't take drugs," I replied. "I don't like pills. I don't even take over-the-counter headache pills. I rarely drink alcohol, beyond a glass of wine with dinner."

"Well," he said, spreading his hands, "consider the prescription just a temporary bridge to help you cope with the stress."

"I suppose in that case," I said, "I can make an exception."

His face softened. "Sam, you're a great attorney," he said. "Look how you saved George Tilson's financial life when he was about to lose that mansion of his, taking his debt down from 3.8 million dollars to just four hundred grand." He could easily afford $400,000.

He snorted. "Hell, he would've been duck soup without you."

I froze. That was confidential information. "My dad told you about that?" I was aware of the grimace on my face, but I didn't care.

"Of course," he said, with a wave of his hand. "Don't worry, the story stops here. People confide in me all the time, Sam. It comes with the territory."

He pointed his index finger at my chest. "Now, get out there and do what you do best."

I stopped at the door. "I was doing what I do best, and look where it got me. Your office!"

"Well, it sounds like you might have missed some of the steps," he said. "I'm just trying to help you help yourself." He smiled. "I want to see you once a week for a while,"

"And, Sam, you need to come up with a goal," he said. "Something you can put some action behind to get you out of this downward emotional spiral. It can be any goal. I don't care if it's the right one, just some goal. You need to do something, even if it's wrong."

We shook hands. I turned to leave. On the inside of his office door was a big sign: 'DOES IT REALLY MATTER?'

I thought about it all the way to my car.

That evening in my tiny apartment, I lay in bed for hours feeling terribly alone. My wife was gone. My business was gone. But mostly, I missed the kids. I wanted to call them, but it was too late at night.

On the way home I had bought the medication Dr. Sid had prescribed. I knew I wouldn't take the pills. I just could not believe I was so bad off that I needed drugs or medication.

Drugs were for hypochondriacs or drug addicts, people who made up all their problems just so they could take drugs. I didn't need drugs.

I rolled over and thrashed under the sheet yet again. "And by the way, Dr. Sid," I shouted, "what kind of advice is that, 'you need to do something, even if it's wrong!?'"

The money situation had really started to bother me. If Cindy made an issue of the proceeds from the sale of the house, I was in trouble.

Then it struck me: Dr. Sid had mentioned disability insurance. I leapt out of bed and dragged my file boxes and personal papers to the kitchen table.

I found the policy and read and reread the clause about nervous disorders to be sure of the criteria for qualification of benefits: "A nervous disorder which denies the insured's ability to perform his/her usual and customary job duties."

That fit my situation. Pretty much.

It made me think of meeting Johnny Redman at the Venice Beach Café many years earlier. Johnny the Rat, they called him, the redhead rat bastard from the east coast.

The cartoon name fit him, with his full head of sleek red hair, his bright eyes, that long nose and pasty white skin.

Johnny had been perceptive, bright, and a fantastic golfer. The PGA tour was his dream. But he just couldn't help shilling, cutting corners, working a con. He had never lost his confidence skills—or his rat sense for survival.

I had asked him once what he did at his boiler room office supply sales job. "I'm a thief selling shit to idiots—you know, like politicians and other B.S. role models," he had said, straight-faced.

"I have a case for you, Sam," he'd told me one time. That had worried me. This is the scariest phrase known to lawyers. It means the person wants you to work for free, or at best for a percentage of something that is really nothing.

Johnny had purchased a disability insurance policy. The policy would pay $2,500 per month for a fixed number of years. But it would still allow him to do other things, like play golf, without losing his benefits.

While disabled, he wouldn't have to make payments on the policy. He just couldn't do the same work that had resulted in his disability. That meant that he could collect disability insurance and still go on the PGA tour.

That was what he had in mind. Even if he placed as low

as fortieth, he could still have fun and keep earning a hundred grand a year when he totaled up his winnings. He could be a professional golfer and have someone else pay the expenses.

I could see his little rat brain working away. How could he get away with it, without getting busted for insurance fraud? He had no concerns about the fact that it was a crime. The only crime was being caught and prosecuted.

Of course I told him to forget about it, but did he listen? No, because he was Johnny the Rat all the way.

He asked me how to file the claim and what the insurance company would do to evaluate him.

I said it would be best if he just got another job. "Insurance companies don't make money by giving it away because you tell them you're disabled," I told him. "They have radar for these types of claims."

Johnny told me he could win the claim if he played the game by the insurance company's rules. He just needed to know what the rules were.

I gave him the same information he would have heard at any seminar on insurance claims.

"They'll speak with your employer, look at all of your available medical records, and make you undergo a physical and psychological examination, be evaluated by a job rehabilitation expert, and answer lots of questions, both verbal and written."

Being a bit nervous and neurotic, Johnny suffered from irritable bowel syndrome, better known as IBS. He hadn't wanted anybody to know that, and had managed to keep it out of his medical record. When he bailed on his job and filed the claim for disability, he used the IBS as the reason.

That turned out to be enough. The claim was investigated, and the examination confirmed his condition. Since there was no prior medical record of it, the insurance company began paying him $2,500 a month. That's why he was called Johnny the Rat.

Johnny went to the golf course. He played on the PGA tour for some years, invested wisely in California real estate, and then secured a high-paying job in, of all things, the insurance industry—investigating fraudulent claims. He always did land on his feet.

Years later, I was able to get fraud work for insurance companies based on the education I received from that redhead rat bastard.

I hadn't represented Johnny the Rat, nor had I taken any money from him. We had merely met occasionally at the local cafés on Ocean Front Walk in Venice Beach, where he would ask me questions, smile, and then skate away.

Seeing how he lived was like watching a film noir crime (who done it) mystery from the 1950s and I found it a bit disturbing. My suburbanite reality had not prepared me for it. Being around someone with an almost fearless sociopathic drive to win at the expense of other people gave me an otherworldly feeling.

Closing the file box, I went back to bed a little more relaxed. I had done something constructive. I had found a source of income that didn't require stress or arguments or dealing with partners.

First thing in the morning, I would call the insurance company and file a claim for disability benefits.

It was four o'clock in the morning, but I still couldn't sleep. My mind was wound up. I tossed and turned some more. Then an idea hit me, and I sat up with a grin on my face.

Dr. Sid wanted me to create a goal. Well, I had a good one: stop that damn dog from barking! I didn't want to hurt him, of course, just mellow him out a little. Calm him down.

Clearly, that nonstop-barking dog needed my prescription pills for his nervous barking disorder more than I needed them.

I threw some clothes on.

Creeping past the pool in my black jeans and black T-shirt, I heard voices in the Jacuzzi. In the darkness, I could barely make out the dark angel and some guy, pressed against the side of the spa.

"Tommy, stop moving," she murmured. "Be a good boy, now. Hush."

Not wanting to disturb them, I sneaked across the deck until I was standing under Mrs. Larson's balcony. I could see the dog dishes by the railing.

As quietly as I could, I pulled a chaise lounge over and climbed up on it. Fully extended, I was still two feet short of the balcony.

I grabbed a lawn chair and set it on the chaise lounge. I climbed up on the chaise lounge and tested the plastic chair.

This was bordering on irrational, but I was determined.

Carefully, I knelt on the seat of the chair. It wobbled a little, but felt fairly stable if I kept my weight in the middle.

Very slowly, I raised first one foot and then the other onto the seat of the chair, and stood. Gingerly, I reached up and grabbed the edge of the concrete balcony to steady myself.

I felt like a combination acrobat and cat burglar.

I pulled the pill bottle out of my jeans pocket and reached a cautious hand over the edge. The metal bowl banged against the railing. I froze.

Visions raced through my brain: lights coming on, angry voices shouting accusations, me being led away in handcuffs, my shame and humiliation knowing no bounds.

But all I could hear was a soft, "Oh, oh, oh," coming from the spa.

Again I stretched out as far as I could, straining to tip the pill bottle into the dog dish. My legs began to twitch. My calves were cramping.

The chair started to chug from side to side under my sneakers. Finally I felt the edge of the dish and tilted the bottle toward it.

At that moment, the dark angel hit her peak. She moaned. The chair flew sideways out from under me. Pills dumped into the dog's dish and clattered across the deck.

I tumbled backward down onto the chaise lounge, bounced straight back up, and landed square on my feet almost as if I had meant to do it.

I hurried to set the chair upright and scurried back across

the deck and up to my apartment.

I fell right to sleep and slept like a rock in a sock for two hours. I woke up thinking about the day James and I had signed our agreement. My mind refused to relent after that, and I tossed and turned for hours before succumbing again to slumber.

7

The nicest thing about not planning is that failure comes as a complete surprise and is not preceded by a period of anxiety.

—*John Preston*

I woke in the morning in good spirits in spite of my lack of sleep, pleased with myself for having taken decisive action toward my goal: Mellowing The Dog.

I had formulated a plan and prepared to advance it. On top of that, I had the disability insurance policy on the table, ready to call and begin my claim process.

And there was something else. I was onto something, but I wasn't sure what it was.

During the sleepless hours of the night my mind had gone over and over the details of the day James had become an official partner in the firm.

James and I had met in my office to sign the two originals. James had taken his for his file, and I'd given him mine to put in our office file. If James had pulled a fast one, how would he have done it? I wracked my brain.

I didn't know what it was, but a voice inside me kept saying there was something I had missed. What was it?

Just before drifting off to sleep I thought of my friend Wayne, my computer technician for the last four years.

Wayne took care of the office computers as well. I hadn't even called him to tell him I'd been ousted from the firm, I realized. I'd have to call him in the morning. When I called him, he had already heard the news.

"I know," he said. "I've been meaning to call you, but I've been so damn busy. James's assistant, what's her name? Annalee? Anyway, she called me to come in and do the quarterly maintenance. I asked about you, of course, and she told me you weren't with the firm anymore. What happened?"

I explained the situation to him.

"You've got to be kidding," he said. "James can't run that office without you. You know that. Am I right?"

"Of course," I said. "But right now I'm locked out, and I don't know how I'm going to rectify that."

I explained about the clause in the agreement saying that all the assets, including my client list, went to James on dissolution of the partnership.

"That's incredible!" Wayne exclaimed. "I smell foul play."

"Me too, but I haven't figured it out. Any ideas?"

"Let me take a look at the email history when I go in next week," Wayne offered. "I'll check the intra-office communications for the week before James was made a partner and for thirty days afterward."

"You can do that?"

"Oh yeah. And since you're the one listed in my files as the owner of the computer, you can authorize me to look at the hard drive while I'm in there. You never know what I might find."

"Well, consider yourself authorized. Let me know if you find anything of interest."

This was questionable procedure, I realized, since I had been ousted from the firm. But I decided to let him run with it. If there was evidence to be found, I needed him to find it.

"Oh, don't worry, I will. If there's anything to find, you'll be hearing from me."

We finished our conversation, catching up on the meaningful details of each other's lives, and hung up.

I poured a glass of orange juice and took it out on my balcony to the little two-seat table with a view of the pool. No one was there yet, and I wanted to enjoy the sound of silence.

Rays of sunshine streaming through the few floating clouds lit the area beautifully. The potted palm trees and lush planter foliage offered a stark green contrast to the bright white walls of the buildings.

The pool glowed a crystal blue, so inviting I considered trying to find my trunks.

Mrs. Larson's balcony was empty. I hoped the dog was asleep. It worried me that too many pills had fallen into his dish.

I had only wanted the dog to stop barking, not die. I pulled the empty pill bottle out of my jeans pocket and set it on the table.

The memory of my climb up to the balcony the previous

night brought a smile to my face. I drank some orange juice, thinking how I had bounced right up off the chaise lounge like some Olympic gymnast.

I turned the bottle around and took a casual glance at the label. I first saw the name of the medication, *"Upsiedaisy-downs,"* and then the caveat.

> *WARNING: May cause emotional disorder of a god-like superiority to others. Behavior demonstrating there is no venue larger than your ego. Most outbreaks are temporary and disappear once patient realizes the necessity of a job to pay mortgage or rent and installment debt. In cases of reoccurrence, notify your healthcare provider immediately.*

Oops! It had never occurred to me that Dr. Sid had given me anything but a mild tranquilizer, a sedative, something to relax me.

Horrified, I stood up and leaned far out over the wrought iron railing to catch sight of Mrs. Larson's entire balcony. Too late! The dog's dish was empty!

"What have I done?" I said out loud, holding my head in my hands. I looked again and almost collapsed.

The dog was out on the balcony. He had somehow leapt up and balanced himself on the top railing of the second-story balcony, head drooping toward the concrete deck below, ears hanging low, eyes downcast. His whole demeanor radiated despair.

"Don't jump!" I shouted. I raced downstairs, taking the

steps two at a time. Running past the pool area, I called out again, "Don't jump! It's not worth it!"

Mrs. Larson's sliding glass door flew open. She ran out onto the balcony screaming, "Sparky! Oh, Sparky!"

I dashed across the pool deck, pleading the whole way for him not to jump, to no avail.

Before I could get under him, the dog looked at me with baleful eyes and dove off the balcony railing. He plummeted toward the concrete, but by some miracle landed on the same cushioned chaise lounge at the poolside that I had set the chair on the night before.

As I gazed in petrified silence, the dog bounced off the chaise lounge and soared high into the air. Reaching the peak of its giant arc, the little body stretched out like an Olympic high board diver. Finally he splashed down into the deep end of the pool.

Mrs. Larson fell back against the balcony wall in a near faint, head down, hands fluttering over her chest like she was having a heart attack.

I ran to the pool utility shed, where the long-handled net for scooping out leaves leaned against the wall. It was about fifteen feet long and awkward to maneuver.

In my panic to save the dog, I failed to turn in time to get it out the door. The pole wobbled uncontrollably and kept banging on the metal shed, making a terrible racket.

I finally wrangled it out, and the net got hung up on a giant palm leaf overhanging the utility shed. I pulled it loose and swung around to the pool, barely keeping my footing, and then walked it carefully over to the edge.

The dog floated mid-pool, not moving. I was sure he was dead. In that moment, I thought my life was over. USA Today headlines would scream, "Disgruntled Lawyer Kills Neighbor's Dog in Unrelenting Barking Dispute."

Cable news channel talking heads would demand an investigation by the ASPCA. Dog blogs would cry out for justice. Mrs. Larson would sue me and I would have to move out, and no decent woman would ever speak to me again.

Stretching the wobbly pole out as far over the water as I could, I managed a tentative bump against the floating body.

The dog sneezed.

"You're alive?" I called out.

The dog slowly raised his head. Trying to focus through blurry eyes, he paddled slowly away, just out of reach.

"Sparky?" Mrs. Larson cried out, draped over her balcony railing. "Is he breathing?"

"Yes," I called back to her. "I'm trying to pull him in."

"Oh, thank God!" she gasped.

I kept pawing at the woozy mutt as he chugged around the pool. At last I succeeded in fishing him out. He was so light the pole didn't even bend.

"What does this dog weigh?" I asked of no one in particular. "Four ounces?" Reeling him in, I took the wet little guy in my hands. "What's wrong with you, Sparky?" I demanded. "You know you're not supposed to eat anything strangers give you."

Sparky licked my hand and gazed sweetly into my eyes.

He seemed to be coming around, perfectly happy to be carried. I grabbed a towel someone had left on a deck chair and dried the dog on my way upstairs.

Mrs. Larson flung the front door open, arms held wide, and smothered the little thing in baby talk and kisses. "Oh, Sam," she gushed. "I can't thank you enough for your bravery and quick thinking."

I told her, "I saw what happened, Mrs. Larson. I did what I had to. Poor little guy. I'm just glad he's all right."

"The late Mr. Larson dearly loved this dog," she said. "I simply couldn't stand it if anything happened to him." She shook a finger at the dog. "Sparky, you naughty boy! What were you thinking?"

The dog's face was covered with her blotchy red lipstick. She turned to me, eyes wide. "That's what Mr. Larson always called the dog. Sparky."

I tried to sound knowledgeable and concerned. Concerned wasn't difficult, for that I was, though more for my good name than for the dog's well being.

But knowledgeable was a stretch. "You might want to take Sparky to the vet, Mrs. Larson, just to be sure."

"I'll do that very thing," she said. "Oh, Sam, you're my hero. I just want to give you a big kiss!"

For the sake of my reputation and to keep my evil secret safe, I endured her giant sloppy kiss. With all the greasy makeup she had on, it felt like being cheek to cheek with a circus clown.

"I'm just glad Sparky is okay," I said, backing away.

She waved a little fingertip goodbye and closed her door. I stumped back down the stairs, feeling enormously relieved I hadn't killed her dog.

As I crossed the deck back to my apartment the dark angel appeared carrying a backpack. Never breaking stride or looking at me, she whispered, "You dropped these," and slipped a baggie into my hand as she glided away to the front gate.

I looked down at my hand. It was all the loose pills I had spilled on the first-floor concrete deck in the darkness of the morning.

I spent the next ten minutes in the bathroom, washing Mrs. Larson's lipstick and makeup off my face.

I did have to smile, now that it was all over. What a break! The pool water had sobered up Sparky, and I, the perpetrator, had managed to rescue the mutt and return him to his owner, safe and sound. I was off the hook.

That put me in a good mood.

Now, to start work on my disability insurance claim. I wrote down the contact number and looked around for my cell phone.

The best things in life are free- But you can keep them for the birds and bees- Now give me money (that's what I want)! Guess who? I opened the phone. "Weisman Dog Rescue."

"Sam," he launched, ignoring my humor. "Have you called Alfonso back yet?"

I sighed. "Not yet, I've been busy. I'll get back to him."

"Well, be sure you do. You're making me look bad."

I didn't answer.

"Listen," he went on, "I need your help."

My heart sank. I knew what was next.

"I have a court thing coming up," he went on. "I need you to handle it for one of my partnerships."

"I'm not doing it for free," I said.

"Don't worry. The partners will take care of you."

"I've got to have a signed legal services agreement and a deposit up front."

Slight pause, then he said, "I'm your father."

"But your partners are not." I didn't want to give in. "When is the court date?"

"Next Friday."

I blew up. "Are you kidding?" I yelled. "It takes sixty days to organize and prepare for a trial!"

"Oh, it's not a trial," he said. "It's just a stupid little arbitration. You can do it in your sleep. Hey, you're going to make money off this. Meet me in an hour."

And he hung up.

I eased the phone shut. "I'm going to make money?" I said to myself. "Worthless last words."

Forty-five minutes later, I pulled into the parking lot of the neighborhood coffee shop, his favorite place for business meetings.

"I will not get bothered or angry," I repeated to myself, reciting affirmations. "I will remain confident and relaxed. Breathe in, and release. Think about whales swimming through deep blue-green waters. Everything around me is cool and refreshing and peaceful. Calm, calm, calm. Tranquil. I am in control. Nothing disturbs me. I remain centered."

I had to jam on the brakes to avoid hitting the concrete parking space bumper. I locked the car and went in. The hostess greeted me. "Table for one?"

Wouldn't that be nice? "No, I'm looking for someone."

"Sam! Sam!" My father hollered, waving at me from a booth by the window as if there were no one else in the restaurant. "Over here. Hurry up!" Customers looked up and then returned to their food.

I felt my body stiffen and the blood rush to my face. I knew my cheeks were beet red as I slunk over to his table. So much for confident and relaxed.

"Sit down," he directed, digging around in his briefcase in a flurry of activity and chaotic disorder.

I sat.

The waitress appeared. My father was not paying attention, so I ordered for both of us. Given that we always have the same thing, that was no big challenge. She left.

The table was covered with plat maps, contracts all marked up in blue and red, architectural plans, and folded yellow legal pads filled with his scribbles.

"What is all this?" I asked.

He looked at me as though I had spoken in Mandarin Chinese. "These are all the documents for my case. What do you think they are?"

When I didn't answer, he went on. "Okay, look at this." He shoved some papers at me. "Now this—here, look at this. No, wait, look at this." One after another, he shuffled through his pile of documents, notes, and maps.

"Dad, I have no idea what you're showing me."

"It's very simple," he said gruffly. "I have a real estate development in East San Diego County: twenty homes, fifteen investors. The prospectus offered riparian land, meaning water running through the development."

He coughed. "I promised to build a green belt – you know, a communal park and walking area along the water. It's an environment thing."

"Yes?" I motioned for him to go on.

"The plans show the creek on the northeast side, here. But with all the rain and the flooding, the water now runs through the southwest end, here." He pointed these out on the map.

"The investors are mad because we can't build homes on the southwest side. They sued me as general partner and want their investment back, plus interest. I could lose about a million dollars."

"I see," I said.

He started shoving papers into an accordion folder. "I need you to make them understand that this can be fixed."

"How am I supposed to do that?"

"I don't know," he gestured with a shrug, holding both hands palms up in front of him. "That's your job." Then he pointed an accusing finger at me. "And make sure you call Alfonso back. It's important."

"It's always important," I muttered under my breath.

The waitress showed up pushing a food cart piled with multiple plates of pancakes, sausage, eggs, hash brown potatoes, and eight plates of toast. Arching an eyebrow, she looked at me. "Wheat toast, right?"

"What is that?" I asked, my eyes glued to the massive array of food on the cart.

"It's your order."

"I didn't order all this," I pleaded, stunned.

Unloading the cart onto our table, she tilted her head toward my father. "The gentleman ordered for the two of you before you came in."

My father beamed. If he'd been wearing suspenders, he would have stuck his thumbs in the straps. "You see," he beamed, "I am a gentleman." He looked at the waitress and said, "Thank you, Marie." She smiled and walked away, shaking her head.

On the drive home it was an effort to keep my eyes on the road. My stomach bulged like a balloon from eating too much and from dealing with my father.

All I could think of was how disorganized he was, how little he'd given me to go on. How was I going to defend him and collect my fee?

My cell phone rang. I didn't recognize the number, and I almost let it go. Then it occurred to me this was the only business line I had now. Pulling off the road, I put on my best legal voice. "Sam Weisman, attorney at law."

"Hello?" I didn't recognize the man's voice. "Is this Sam Weisman?"

"Yes," I said. "To whom am I speaking?"

"My name is Brian Tate," he said. "I found this business

card in my pocket after my car accident last week, and it says 'Witness' on the back. I just wondered if you were the guy who called 911 for me."

"Why, yes, Mr. Tate. I just wanted to make sure you would be all right, and if you had any questions you could call me."

"Oh, you have no idea how grateful I am," he said, relieved. "I stopped for the red light, then BAM! I was hurt pretty bad. I have neck and back injuries. I got disoriented and really didn't know where I was.

"The girl who ran into me," he went on, "who was clearly at fault by the way, won't answer my calls. I've left messages on her voicemail regarding her insurance information, but no response. Anyway, my car is in the repair shop. The rental car bill is getting big, and so are my medical expenses."

"That's not good," I sympathized.

"Well, no, it's not," he replied. "My insurance agent said I should hire an attorney. So, you're a lawyer then?"

"That I am," I said with confidence.

"You were there," he said. "But I guess you need to know some more from my doctor. Can you take my case?"

I hesitated only briefly, pondering the ethics of this. To avoid conflict of interest, an attorney who has witnessed an accident should not solicit business from either party. I had written 'Witness' on the card, but in fact I had not seen the crash.

I grabbed my notebook and a pen to make notes.

"Tell you what, Mr. Tate," I said. "Let's meet this week, maybe Friday if that's okay with you. Bring everything—the police report, your doctor bills and medicine bills, the car rental bills, an estimate of your car repair costs—just whatever you have, and I'll review your case. The first consultation is, of course, free of charge."

We agreed on a time and a place to meet. He sounded very pleased by the time we hung up. I closed my notebook with a triumphant slap and drove home with a smile on my face.

8

> Be who you are and say what you feel,
> because those who mind don't matter
> and those who matter don't mind.
>
> —*Dr. Seuss*

The poolside lay deserted in the early morning, allowing me ample solitude for reflection. I returned to my apartment clear headed and excited after an early morning swim. I had a new case.

Yes, I had to organize and prepare for my father's arbitration, but I would get to that soon. There were some other matters I had to deal with, too, like the divorce. But things were looking up.

I showered, shaved, dressed, and headed to the kitchen table to start my work day. I checked the cell phone voice mail. There were three messages. The first number was one I didn't recognize. I pushed the button.

"Mr. Weisman, this is Roger Chapman of Wiezel, Cheatham and Howard. I represent James Watkins in the partnership lawsuit. I'm calling about the Status Conference for next Tuesday to determine whether this matter can be sent to arbitration or we have to go to trial.

"I don't need to tell you how much a trial will cost you, besides having to pay my attorney fees and costs. I need to know if you are going to take any depositions, and if so how many, or whether you're planning to delay this matter in any other manner.

"I want to be prepared to tell the judge how James's case is proceeding. So, how are you doing? Can we proceed in reliance upon your cooperation? Please call me back at your first convenience."

Damn. I hadn't finished filling out my Status Conference Report. The Status Conference judge was not going to be happy if I wasn't prepared.

The whole thing made me mad. With so much going on in my life now, I had not given a thought to hiring an attorney.

And then I had an illumination: I knew more about my practice than any attorney I could bring in. I was more familiar with all the ins and outs of my business than anyone. I had built that law firm from the ground up, long before James had joined.

I was the one who developed all the clientele; who set up the organization; who laid the foundation of the firm. James had only enjoyed the fruits of all my hard work.

I would represent myself. What could possibly go wrong? Yes, I'd jumped all over the guy at the restaurant for doing that, but he wasn't an attorney. I was.

Fired up with righteous anger, I stood straight and aimed my accusing finger across an imaginary courtroom at that conniving villain, James "The Ripper" Watkins.

After making a note to call Chapman back, I played the second message: "Hey, Sam, it's Alfonso Lechuga, the friend of your dad from the plastics industry. Just getting back to you again. I talked to Ben and I understand you're very busy. Give me a ring when you can."

He always ended his calls with that same happy tone. The guy was terminally cheerful. I could not imagine what he wanted me to do for him. I deleted the message.

It was time to call Amelia. After the dinner escapade I wasn't sure she'd want to see me again, but I definitely wanted to see her. Time to show her that I wasn't always so close to being over the edge.

And besides, I thought she'd probably like to know I'd followed her suggestion.

I dialed her number.

"MesoAmerican Leasing, this is Amelia Lopez," she intoned in her gentle business voice. If I needed a pick-me-up, this was it.

"Hi, Amelia," I said. "It's Sam."

"Oh, Sam!" She sounded startled. "Can I call you right back?"

Concerned, I said, "Of course."

"Thanks, bye."

Just like that, she was gone.

My pick-me-up had turned into a let-me-down. What had happened? I stared out my front window as if expecting an asteroid to crash into the earth, obliterating life as we know it.

The phone rang. It startled me so I almost dropped it. I hurried to flip it open.

"Hello?"

"Sam, it's Amelia." Her voice sounded cheery, nothing like the voice that had hung up on me. "I'm so sorry for putting you off before. I was with a leasing client. It's a big account and I have to pamper them, you know?"

"Oh, yes," I said, recovering quickly. "I understand client management only too well. They complain constantly about their situation. We have to hold their hand and tell them everything will be all right." I laughed. "As you and I know, it's not a hobby."

"If it was a hobby," she said, not missing a beat, "I would be on the beach under a cabana with a piña colada and my cell phone, and let someone else run from property to property in heavy traffic."

She paused, and her tone softened. "Sam, I'm happy to hear your voice again."

"Me too," I said. "Happy to hear your voice."

"I had a good time the other night. I was a little concerned about you, though. Tell me, did you go see Dr. Sid?"

"Yes, actually I did," I said, basking now in the memory of the warm glow of her presence.

"And how was it? Did it help?"

"Everything went great," I said. "Much better than I expected. I don't know why I was so apprehensive. Dr. Sid and I talked about old times and had a great session. He reminded me that I am a good attorney and just need to get back on the horse that threw me. I told him I had a whole stable of horses."

"A whole stable?" she said, playing coy. "My, aren't you the stallion."

"All right, maybe not a whole stable." We shared a laugh. "He did tell me I needed to set a goal," I went on. "And he said going out with you is good for me."

"Oh, he did not," she giggled. "I don't believe you."

"He said you would help me get back on track."

She paused a moment before replying. "I would like to see you again, Sam." Her voice flowed over me like a warm bath. "Let's have dinner again, but this time I pick the restaurant."

"Mexican, right?" I asked.

"Sí, como no?" she laughed, delightedly. "Of course, but this will be Veracruz style. You will like it."

"I can't wait," I said.

The front gate buzzer startled me.

"I have to go," I told Amelia. We made a quick date for Saturday and hung up. I pressed the intercom button.

"Sam Weisman, who is it?"

"*She loves you, yeah, yeah, yeah…*" Whoever had lived here before had rigged the intercom to play the Beatles.

"Come in, Diane." I hit the buzzer to let her in.

"I have Mom with me," her voice came back.

I punched the button again. "Hi, Mom. Come on in. Walk through the main entry till you see the pool. Go past the pool to Building Two. I'm on the second floor, apartment 223."

"Thank you, dear." Her voice carried that sweet even-tempered Mom tone.

I buzzed them in and went out onto the balcony. They were passing the mailboxes when I got to the railing.

Our mailman, clad in his full USPS uniform and leather satchel, was busy stuffing junk mail and magazines into the slots.

"Up here, Mom!" I waved them over to the elevator. Mrs. Larson's balcony was empty, I noticed. The curtain had been pulled across the sliding glass doors.

"Hey, Sam!" I looked down by the gate to see my neighbor waving up at me.

Bill White was a brilliant but eccentric astrophysicist who commuted to the Jet Propulsion Laboratories in the foothills of Pasadena two weeks a month.

He and his wife Wendy were renting at the complex while they completed construction on their seaside dream home on a hill overlooking the Pacific Ocean.

Bill had asked me to look over some loan documents for them.

"Construction's almost done," Bill shouted up, shading his eyes with his hand. "We'll be moving in soon!"

"That's great," I waved back. "I'd love to see it when it's finished."

Bill saluted and pulled on his wide brim hat with the bandanna tucked around the back to protect his neck, like a French Foreign Legion helmet. Dressed in long pants and a long-sleeved shirt, he drew on gloves and sunglasses and marched off through the gate to take his daily walk—in eighty-nine-degree heat. Bill was scared to death of skin cancer.

Why he bought everything at Discount Don's Clothing Emporium when he could easily afford Neiman Marcus was beyond me.

I waited by the elevator, wondering what was taking Diane and my mother so long. They appeared at last at the top of the staircase.

"I thought you'd be on the elevator, Mom," I said.

"I'm not decrepit yet," she sniffed. I glanced at my sister. Her eyebrows went up, but neither of us said anything. I hugged my mother.

"I just wanted to see how you were doing," she said.

"I'm great, Mom," I replied. What I meant was, so far, so good. But of course it was still only morning. Anything could happen. I led them down the hall. "Let me show you the apartment," I said.

My mother was really a dear heart. My father had met her in England when he was in the Army during World War II. He'd married her at the end of the war and brought her back home to snowy cold New York. After a few years they moved out west to enjoy the good life in sunny southern California.

Like many people who had survived the Great Depression and the war, he wanted a better life with a family, a good income, and no snow.

He succeeded at all of that, thanks in no small part to his ever patient, quietly efficient wife. He became the proud father of a son and a daughter, a lawyer and a finance specialist.

Inside the apartment, I showed them around. "Large rooms," I said with a mixture of pride and disgust, "and for the moment at least, a clean bathroom and kitchen.

"It's very nice, Sam," Mom said with an approving nod.

She peered at me with that x-ray vision mothers have. It penetrates every secret corner of your soul, exposes all your sins, reveals every snag, difficulty or trouble you've been having.

I don't know how they do it, but they all can.

She went on, "Since you don't have a housekeeper anymore, who's taking care of your laundry?"

I had to laugh. "I send it out, Mom."

Diane gazed at the walls. "Brilliant décor," she deadpanned. "Who's your designer?"

"Yeah, right. I guess you think it needs a woman's touch." Not a bad idea, I registered.

"Maybe. But only the right woman's."

"Right!" I agreed. "Would you two like some refreshments? I have some iced tea from the refrigerator."

"That sounds nice," my mother said. "And do you have anything else? Like maybe some donuts? Or sweet rolls?"

I shook my head. "Don't you know that stuff sticks in your colon for twenty years?"

"What's your suggestion, doctor?" Diane asked. I couldn't be sure whether her expression was a frown or a smirk. "Health food snacks?"

"Well, actually, yes." I reached into a cupboard. "Organic health food cookies."

"Where did you get these?"

"Dr. Sid gave me a package," I replied. "Have some."

Mom reached into the bag. "Thank you." She took two and looked up at me again with penetrating eyes. "Tell Sidney hello for me."

Diane picked up the cookie bag. "Maybe we can go sit by the pool?"

"That's an excellent idea," our mother said. "Sam can show us the rest of the complex, and we can sit and relax."

I led them out for a tour. My sister Diane cast an apprais-ing glance as we entered the pool area, taking it all in.

Astute, perceptive, self-possessed and condescending by nature, my sister's saving grace was her sarcastic wit.

Diane had a good academic brain and had developed into a smart businessperson. She was tough; sometimes she gave the impression she ate nails for breakfast.

She could be nice and loving, like the time she'd agreed to watch our kids when Cindy and I went out of town, but such times were few and far between.

In that respect she took after our father. She got what she wanted. Always. Especially from our father.

Her poor husband hadn't stood a chance; they had played by her rules. He'd needed a hall pass just to spend an evening out with his friends. After living under house arrest for too many years, he had finally pulled up stakes.

Diane hadn't seemed too bothered; I think she figured there were more fish in the sea.

"So, Sam," Diane said, motioning with her head toward

the pool area. "What's with the No Nude Swimming sign? Did they put that up just for you?"

My mother grimaced at her. "Diane, behave yourself."

"Well, I'm just remembering a certain high school episode...." Her face had that evil teasing grin I loved and hated.

Mom turned back to me. "Is your father hounding you again?"

"So what's new?"

"Be sure you don't take him too seriously," she said. "His bark is worse than his bite."

"Yeah," my sister snorted, "like a rabid Doberman Pinscher."

"How are you taking the divorce?" my mother asked gently.

"I'm all right, for the moment," I shrugged. "Cindy's attorney got a court order for me to pay all the bills and the mortgage. She told the judge it's in the best interest of the children."

"You've got wonderful children, Sam," she said.

On the heels of that thought came one that clouded her expression. "I don't know how they turned out so well. I'm sorry, I know I shouldn't say this, but I can't help it, because it's true—Sam, I know your father's crazy about her, but for my part I never thought Cindy was the right wife for you."

"Oh, no?" Diane chided. "Good enough for Sports Illustrated, but not right for Sam?" Sports Illustrated was Cindy's one claim to fame. The summer before we got married, her picture had been on the back cover of the famous swimsuit edition.

Diane turned her attention to me. "So… what is she asking for in the settlement? Is she leaving you anything?"

"You know," I hedged. "We're working it out."

My mother gave me one of those looks I recognized as an indication she was not going to allow me to hold her off. "Sam, tell me what's going on."

I relented. "Cindy asked for two hundred and fifty grand out of my portion of the proceeds after escrow. She told me she needs it to pay off family debts so she can qualify for the mortgage on her new house. She says it's for the sake of the children."

"You can't be serious," my mother said. "Did you question her about it?"

"Well, not really," I admitted. "Dealing with women who want something from me on a personal level has never been my strong suit."

"You always got what you wanted from me," Diane teased.

"Yeah, right. So who always ended up with the best skates when we were kids? The nicest bike?" I gave a gentle tug on a dangling strand of her hair. "Who didn't have to stay home and entertain the pool guests?"

"I would have boxed your ears if you hadn't let me go play. And you're right, you never were very good at defending yourself against a girl. So how are you going to protect yourself against this one?"

"I got her to sign a promissory note with a Deed of Trust on the new house."

Diane looked grave. "Have you recorded it yet?"

"Not yet," I said. "She told me to hold it for a few days so she can get all her paperwork together."

"You should have done that right away," she said, looking displeased. "You know you can't keep your brain in gear when it comes to dealing with her."

"Look, Diane…" I was getting my back up. "It's going to be okay. I've been through the new house and it's worth what she's paying. My only concern is for the kids. The place feels cold and unwelcoming. She has furniture in her room, but the kids are still waiting."

"What?" my mother looked shocked. "Your children don't deserve that."

Diane pressed me. "Do you have copies of the note, and the Deed of Trust, and all your original marriage papers?"

"Of course," I said, doing my best to stay calm.

"Good," she said. "Then maybe it will be okay."

"All I know is, I can't afford to pay for her mistakes," I said. "I can barely afford to pay for my own."

At that moment Mrs. Larson came through the front gate with Sparky in a tiny pet carrier. She wiggled toward us with rapid little mincing steps.

"Oh, Sam," she gushed, "my hero."

She turned to my mother to introduce herself. "Harriet Larson," she said, and put out her free hand. "You must be Sam's mother. Your son saved my Sparky from drowning in the swimming pool."

"How do you do? I'm Elaine Weisman," my mother said

in a warm tone. “This is my daughter, Diane.”

Diane nodded to her.

Mrs. Larson turned her attention on me. “Sam, I took your advice,” she said. “Dr. Gillespie, our family veterinarian, said Sparky is fine. But he has a little acne, and his cholesterol level was a bit high.”

“Oh, really?” I tried to sound sympathetic. “Anything else?”

“Well…” She puckered her brow. “It seems the examination revealed an antidepressant in his bloodstream.”

Diane’s eyebrows shot up two notches. My mother just listened.

Mrs. Larson went on. “Sparky used to be a bad boy and get into Mr. Larson’s medication, but it never seemed to bother the dog.

“It’s confusing because I don’t have a prescription for antidepressants. I do take a mood elevator stimulant, amphetamine something or other.”

She turned to my mother. “I have been rather distressed since my husband died.”

“Oh, I’m sorry to hear that,” my mother said, deeply sympathetic. “How long has it been?”

Mrs. Larson looked at the dog’s paws, almost as if counting claws. “Twenty-three years last February.” She patted Sparky on the back and smiled faintly at my mother.

Neither my mother nor Diane said anything. They looked stunned.

“I just can’t understand why Sparky has been so jumpy

these days."

She's nuts, I thought to myself. Then it came to me, the reason behind the out-of-control barking. Sparky had been eating her medication! The dog was a speed freak!

"Well, it's been very nice to meet the family of Sparky's rescuer," Mrs. Larson said, again shaking my mother's hand. "Please come enjoy the pool anytime."

After she left, Diane prodded me with her elbow. "She makes pulling the dog out of the pool sound like you saved the President's son from a flaming airplane crash."

Out of nowhere the dark angel whispered past. She wore a thin robe that flowed over her as she walked towards the pool.

Diane watched her go by, transfixed as she watched her slowly disrobe to display her string bikini and then climb into the bubbling hot spa.

"Who is that?" she whispered.

"Just one of the tenants." I couldn't keep from grinning.

"Mmm, I can see why you chose this apartment complex over the hundreds of others I know you checked out. Lots of women here to practice defending yourself against."

My mother just sighed. "Take me home, Diane."

We said our goodbyes and my mother and sister stood up to depart. I promised to call home more often.

"Bye, big brother," Diane purred, looking back at me with a wink as she took my mother's elbow to lead her out the gate.

Heading back to my apartment, I wondered how it could be possible for Sparky to have eaten Mr. Larson's meds if he had died twenty-three years earlier. Dogs didn't live that long. It had to be a different dog. Maybe this was Sparky II or III?

Maybe there never was a Mr. Larson? Maybe the woman was a hypochondriac? Who knew?

I had bigger fish to fry at the moment. My Status Conference on Tuesday, for one.

9

> The more real you get,
> the more unreal they are.
> —*John Lennon*

I was feeling sharp and prepared.

On my kitchen table stood an accordion folder containing the partnership documents, files and miscellaneous notes, all neatly organized.

I had carefully filled out my Status Conference Information Questionnaire and stacked it with every other piece of information I would need for the Status Conference at nine o'clock.

This hearing would just be a formality, at the end of which Judge Michael Flores would send us straight to arbitration.

After the discovery was complete, the judge would set a Settlement Conference. I would summarize the case in a brief and hand it to the judge. He would settle the case in my favor and I would be awarded my rightful half of the assets, clients, and receivables.

I would go my way and James would go his. All would be well with the world.

My cell phone rang. "Sam Weisman," I answered.

"Mr. Weisman?" It was a woman's voice. "My name is Roxann Miller. I am a claims representative with Gotcherbach Insurance Claims Services."

"Oh, yes," I said brightly. That was my disability insurance carrier. "I filled out all the forms and submitted them last week."

"That is correct, Mr. Weisman," she said. "We have requested your medical records and are trying to get your employment records from your law firm now. But that is proving difficult, because they have refused to release any information."

I couldn't believe James was blocking my claim.

Roxann went on, "Just now I am calling to make appointments for your physical and psychological evaluations."

I didn't have time for this. "Roxann, I have to be in court in less than an hour—not to represent a client, you understand, but as a party to a lawsuit. May I call you back?"

"This will only take a few minutes," she insisted.

Hadn't she heard me? Did she understand English? I caught myself, got a grip on my rising indignation and held my tongue. "I have your number," I said. "I will get back to you." And closed the phone.

Inhale. Exhale. Again.

I shut my eyes and pictured giant whales floating off the tip of Baja, down by the Sea of Cortez.

It didn't work. All I could think about was the money I had agreed to give Cindy from my portion of the sale. I still hadn't recorded the Deed of Trust in second position to her mortgage to secure and protect my loan to her.

My sister's warning rang in my ears. Why had Cindy asked me to wait until after escrow closed? Was she holding something back?

Driving to the courthouse, I felt rushed. I hated being late, and I knew Judge Flores was adamant about punctuality.

When I arrived at the courthouse, the nearest parking space was so far away I had to hail a taxi to get to the building. I breezed through the front doors and raced up the steps to the second floor and down the hall to the designated room.

This would be an actual court hearing before a judge in a courtroom. There could be as many as twenty cases on the court's conference calendar.

I knew the place would be packed with attorneys, all talking, some conversing to friends, some to opposing counsel, some planning dinners, some talking about the Padres game—all the usual non-legal banter.

It's a good thing the clients don't see this, I thought.

I came in just as the judge was about to take the bench. The bailiff roared like a drill sergeant for everybody to have a seat and remain quiet. I rushed up to hand him my paperwork.

He looked at me sharply. "Go back and take a seat."

"I just want to turn in my questionnaire."

"Go back and take a seat," he said stiffly.

I had no choice. I had to slide between expensive suits, highly polished shoes, two-hundred-dollar ties, and disapproving looks, all the way to the far back corner of the courtroom before I could find a seat.

Judge Flores came in and sat at the bench. He adjusted the microphone and turned to the clerk. "Has everyone given you their information forms?"

"One moment, Your Honor," said the ever efficient Lucy Hernandez. She stood up and faced the room and hollered, "Has everybody handed me their Status Conference Questionnaire Report? If not, bring it to me now."

Dead silence in the room. I was the only one who stood up and waved my form. I navigated through the sea of shiny lawyers to the aisle and took a step forward to the clerk.

Judge Flores boomed over the loudspeaker, "Just hand it to the bailiff, Counselor."

That stopped me in my tracks. I did so and returned to my seat in the back. Once again I had to navigate past all the lawyers, brushing their suits, bumping into their shiny shoes.

"Good morning," Judge Flores boomed. "We have twenty cases today. I hope we won't have any more delays."

He looked at his watch. "I want this over within one hour. Each of you will have less than one minute to speak, if at all necessary." There was some rustling of feet and shuffling of papers, but no one said a word.

The judge called the first case. Two attorneys rose and stepped forward to the Counsel tables while Judge Flores reviewed their questionnaires. He looked up. "Is everything on here correct?"

"Yes, Your Honor," responded both attorneys.

"Are there any discovery requests or motions not listed

that either of you intend to take?"

"No, Your Honor," they said together. "We're ready."

Judge Flores made a note. "Based on your Attorney Reports, this case falls within the arbitration requirements. Therefore this court orders this case to be arbitrated within sixty days of today's date. See the clerk for the arbitration information. Next case."

The attorneys approached the clerk. She handed them each a list of arbitrators to choose from, and out the doors they went.

This went on case after case for nearly an hour, some being set for trial, most going to arbitration. All I could do was sit in the back row and think about Amelia and how good she made me feel.

Why not? It was the best way I knew of to pass the time.

Finally there were only two attorneys left, me and a tall, tanned, perfectly groomed man in the front row wearing a beautiful English suit with gold cufflinks.

This had to be Roger Chapman. With a superior smile, he stood up and waited while I worked my way through the seats and down the aisle.

"Finally, the last case," said Judge Flores, waving to us. "Gentlemen, approach the bench." As we walked up, Judge Flores turned to the clerk. "And I thought I was going to break my record today," he complained.

"Well, Your Honor," said Lucy Hernandez, "close, but no banana. Though you did only miss by four minutes." The judge laughed and picked up our questionnaires.

"Seems to be a fairly simple matter, Mr. Weisman. Based on your information, you only have a couple of depositions to take and some requests for production of documents. Looks like this case belongs in arbitration."

Good. That was just what I thought.

Scanning the other Status Conference Report, the judge looked surprised. He turned to Chapman, "Eighteen depositions, Counselor?"

No way. Who was he going to depose, two baseball teams? Lawyers never lie, except when their lips are moving.

Chapman was unfazed. "We have a lot of witnesses, Your Honor."

Judge Flores kept reading. "Interrogatories, a long list of requests for production of documents that looks more like my wife's grocery list. And what's this about an expert forensic accountant?"

"It's a big, complicated case, Your Honor," Chapman said.

No, it's not, I thought to myself. This was a ploy. Chapman wanted the judge to move the case forward into a time consuming and costly trial, which he knew would pump up my expenses and increase his own billable hours.

Chapman went on. "The accounting, the books and records, all of it has to be investigated going back several years."

The judge tilted his head. "Are you accusing Mr. Weisman of fraud?"

"Your Honor," Chapman said, "we have to dig into the documents before we can make any sort of assessment."

The judge looked back at me. "Mr. Weisman, you obviously disagree. Tell me what the case is about."

Now it was time to show Chapman who he was dealing with. "Your Honor," I said firmly, "it's a simple dissolution of our law firm partnership. I built the law practice, developed the clientele, and created the reputation long before James Watkins came onto the scene."

Chapman horned back in. "Your Honor, my client's claim is that, in the event the partnership is dissolved, my client is entitled to retain all of the assets and property, and he and Mr. Weisman will split all incurred debts and expenses."

The judge just stared at him for a moment, and then turned back to me as if he had suddenly realized I was alone. "Where's your attorney, Mr. Weisman? Why are you here?"

"I'm representing myself, Your Honor."

Chapman chortled.

Judge Flores said to me, "I don't have to tell you what that means."

I kept still.

Judge Flores rubbed his chin, considering. "This case looks to me like an acrimonious and bitter dispute, one in which only the attorneys for the parties will win."

He knew Chapman was just playing lawyer, exaggerating the amount of work required to prepare for the arbitration so that he could extract a bigger fee to pay for his next expensive toy.

I hoped this wouldn't be long and drawn out. We should be in and out of arbitration in two hours.

Judge Flores went on. “I am going to issue an order mandating this case to arbitration, with the hope that it can be settled in a satisfactory manner.”

That made me feel better. Now it was going my way.

“In the meantime,” the judge continued, “the court orders that the parties meet and confer regarding settlement within ten days from the date of this Status Conference.”

What? He had to be kidding! All I wanted was what I had brought to the partnership. That was my settlement. End of discussion!

“And,” Judge Flores said, “the parties will file a Joint Meet and Confer Statement of the results of their Meet and Confer session with this court within thirty days from today, indicating whether or not a settlement has been reached. It is so ordered. All right, we’re done here.”

The judge jogged his papers on the bench top to make them tidy and then looked at me. “You might consider retaining counsel, Mr. Weisman.” He slid the papers back into the file and got up to leave.

Chapman took this opportunity to make a point of his personal relationship with the judge. “How did you like that eighteenth hole at Buckhorn, Mickey?” he asked in a conversational tone.

Judge Flores turned around in delight. “Oh, it’s a real corker!” He made an excited fist. “And I birdied it! We’ll have to play it again, maybe next week.”

Chapman turned to me. “Hey, Weisman, how come you look like you’re in shock?” He stuck the arbitration package into his briefcase and walked away without waiting for an answer.

The judge's order meant I was going to have to deal with Chapman and Watkins. The partnership fight would be unbelievably dragged out.

Lucy Hernandez handed me the arbitration packet.

"Thank you, Mrs. Hernandez," I said. It was a lie. I was far from thankful.

I was sitting at a traffic light on the boulevard when my phone rang. I pulled through the green light and over to the curb.

"Hi, Dad."

"Rachel!" I said, my spirits rising. "Happy to hear from you, but I'm on my way to an appointment."

"Can I talk to you for a minute?"

"Sure," I said. "What is it?"

"Mom hasn't bought my bedroom furniture with the money you gave her yet. My clothes are still in boxes in the garage, and I'm sleeping on the floor on my camping mattress."

Oh, this was not good. "What did your mother say?"

"She said she'll get around to it," Rachel answered. "Dad, Ryan's asthma is really bad. He sneezes day and night, because she used the money to buy these stupid expensive Cornish Rex cats. The breeder told her they were hypoallergenic—whatever that means—but Ryan's miserable. He looks like someone stuck onions on his eyes."

There was a short pause. "I wish you were here," she said. She sounded sad.

"Rachel," I said, "when you come over this weekend, we'll have a cookout and sit around the pool. We can talk then, all right?"

"Can you pick us up so we don't have to listen to Mom complain about driving us over?"

"Sure," I said. "I'll be there at eleven. I'll beep the horn twice."

Rachel giggled. "Two beeps are good for me."

"I'll call you back," I told her. "Try to hang in there."

"Okay." She hung up.

I knew Cindy was doing this because she knew it would bother me. She wanted to make me lose focus. I would fix it somehow, but for the moment my hands were full. I got back on the road.

At last I arrived at Dr. Sid's office. At least here I could relax and enjoy the late morning sun across the ocean's blue-green surface while eating a health food cookie. The perky receptionist was an added plus.

Talking to her, I was captivated by a conversation about beach volleyball or some such thing, I'm not sure what. It didn't matter. All I could see was tan and blonde and white lace.

"Sam!" A familiar voice from another room broke my concentration. "Sam! Stop looking at that girl and come in here!"

I excused myself and went to join Dr. Sid into his office. Taking a seat, he crossed his legs and asked, "So what's happened since we last met?"

There was so much to tell that I went blank. "Do you know anything about Cornish Rex cats?"

He just looked at me. "That's not what's bothering you."

"Well, no, it's not," I said. "What's bothering me is that James is trying to steal my law practice. And Cindy's being selfish, wasting my support money on her indulgences instead of providing for my kids."

Oh, she would have loved that, I'm sure.

He twisted his lips in a quizzical expression. "What do you mean, selfish?"

"I gave Cindy money for the kids and she spent it on Cornish hens—uh, I mean Cornish Rex cats. Expensive thoroughbred cats. My daughter's sleeping on the floor. My son's asthma is getting worse. And all she cares about are those stupid cats."

"Is there more?" he asked.

"Unfortunately." I filled him in on the division of the house sale proceeds and the fact that Cindy wanted two hundred and fifty grand over and above her half. "She has a buyer, and they are in escrow now, waiting to close," I said.

"So, the house has sold already?" he smiled, spreading his hands. "That's good news."

"Well, yes."

He sat up and shot me a sharp look. "Sam, you don't sound excited. You haven't told me the whole story."

"What do you mean?"

"There are times you don't tell the whole story," he said.

"And that's a prescription for failure, in business and in your personal life. This is something we need to talk about more." He sat back. "Have you given her the money already?"

"No," I said. "She gets it at the close of escrow." I folded my arms in frustration. "It was for the good of the children. She said it was in their best interest."

"Sam, you're an attorney," he said evenly. "You deal with your clients' legal problems every day, asking them for proof of what they say. What proof did you have that she would use the money for your children?"

I paused. "She said she would. She's their mother, for Pete's sake."

Dr. Sid put his hands on his knees and looked at me like I was a kid. "I have an assignment for you," he said. "Find a good lawyer to represent you in the divorce."

"Ha!" I cried. "Goal accomplished. My sister's friend, Andrea Diener, is going to handle my case. That's her specialty."

"Good." Dr. Sid brightened. "Because if you represented yourself against your wife, you would have an idiot for an attorney and your attorney would have a schmuck for a client."

"Yeah, yeah, I know." I heaved a deep sigh.

Dr. Sid jumped up and began circling the room, waving his finger. "I have another assignment for you, Sam," he said. "I love that term you came up with—you know, 'bi-chotic.' It just keeps growing in my mind, sprouting all sorts of ideas."

"What do you want me to do?" I asked, feeling somewhat

bewildered.

"Envision a business partnership with me for a whole line of T-shirts with my patients' crazy statements on them. You follow me?"

"Sort of," I managed.

"It could be hugely successful with the upscale therapy crowd, Sam. You know, people at cocktail parties talking about their therapy sessions. Going to therapy is their social event of the day. It could become a fashion statement. The Beverly Hills therapists might even get what the T-shirts mean. What do you think?"

I didn't really know what to think. "Sure, I guess," I said. Who was I to put the brakes on Dr. Sid? "But you'll need to sign a non-compete, non-disclosure, non-circumvention agreement."

"Absolutely," he said, not realizing I was kidding. "Bring it with you to the next session, along with the partnership license agreement. That will be your assignment, to come up with an agreement between us to use the phrases on promotional T-shirts. Make it simple. Fifty-fifty split."

He turned back around to me and put out his hand. "Fair enough?"

I shook his hand. "My mother said to tell you hello," I said.

A warm glow came over his face. "Please give Elaine my best regards. I do miss the old pool days."

On the way out, I couldn't help reading the "DOES IT REALLY MATTER?" sign again.

Driving home along the coast, I said out loud, "I'm a schmuck if I represent myself against Cindy? I thought he said I was a good attorney! Oh, well."

In truth, I knew he was right. It had nothing to do with being a good attorney. It had to do with emotional detachment and objectivity, and with being willing to say no to a woman, even the one I had married.

Especially the one I had married.

I kept glancing over my shoulder at the endless stretch of peaceful blue water. Wouldn't it be nice to nestle down in the warm sand and feel that gentle breeze over my skin? Could I ever take off and get away from it all?

I wished I had a home with an ocean view, like the one Cindy and I had. Or one with a view across any body of water.

Then it struck me. Amelia had said her father owned property in Mexico. Was it anywhere near a large body of water?

I seemed to recall that Veracruz was on the Gulf of Mexico. In my imagination I saw palm trees, a beach, and beautiful mountains in the background.

Why not? I could use my legal skills, and my experience working real estate with my father as well.

I could create a small boutique resort in Mexico for tourists. Package vacations for American tourists, sort of like a cruise ship on land. And in Mexico it would be inexpensive, half the cost of anywhere else. Or even less.

I was getting excited. Yes! I unbuttoned my shirt and loosened my tie.

10

Show me your friends and it will tell me all about you.

—old proverb

Amelia had a late apartment showing, so I agreed to meet her at Boca del Rio. As much as I like Mexican food, I had cut back on my regular visits to Mexican restaurants in recent years to reduce the fat and the calories in my diet.

Amelia assured me Veracruz style was very healthy and natural. I would keep an open mind.

In a moment of luck, I found a parking space right next to the front door. Maybe it was time to stop practicing law and just go to restaurants!

I waited on a bench outside next to the ornate front door, under candlelit coach lanterns, palm leaves and banana trees.

"Sam!"

Amelia's voice had a sweet ring to it, and I jumped to my feet.

"I didn't see you drive up." I said.

"The parking is terrible," she groused. "I am way at the far end of the lot." Then her face broke into a smile that started at the eyes and didn't stop. "Let's go in. I'm ready for a Margarita."

I laughed. "If they have a Mexican Shirley Temple, I'm there." Taking my hand, she led me into the restaurant.

After a short wait we were seated in an almost private alcove under a stone arch, part of the colonial Mexican décor.

The place was inviting, done in earthy tropical colors, historically rustic. Driftwood and beach art pieces hung on the walls. We looked over the menu and crunched little green banana chips in a spicy peanut and garlic sauce.

"I really have no idea what to order," I said. She held up a finger.

Our waiter looked like some kind of Mayan farm hand. Amelia spoke to him in such a flurry of passion, liberally punctuated with hand gestures, that even if I had taken Spanish lessons I couldn't have begun to follow.

He nodded, answered her briefly, and zoomed off to the kitchen.

She turned to me. "Everyone who works here is from Veracruz. I ordered us drinks and some *picadas*—little corn tortillas with avocado and tomatillo sauce."

"Sounds good to me," I said, thinking how painless it was to be with this woman. She eased my mind and made it possible to set aside for a while the avalanche of trouble, reversals, bad luck, and outright meanness that seemed to make up my life lately.

I liked looking at her, especially in this subdued warm light that made her eyes shine. Her mannerisms and gestures came naturally, very feminine. Her voice flowed with a rich, tropical smoothness.

She was telling me how her mother had taught her to cook *huachinango Veracruzana*, Red Snapper Veracruz style, with tiny roasted white potatoes and white rice.

I could only imagine how the family had saved up enough money to buy the fish and then gathered her father's vegetables for a special occasion dinner. I wondered how they got by the rest of the time. She probably sent them money from her leasing job.

"True Veracruz sauce," she said, "has tomatoes, onions, garlic, capers, and green olives. I like to add bay leaves and the juice from jalapeños. That is how I learned to make it back home."

Sitting across the table from Amelia, looking into her eyes and drinking in the melody of her voice, I heard my libido and emotions urging me to put the moves on her.

But it just didn't feel right. It had been a long time since I'd dated anyone, and Amelia made it so effortless I forgot to be anxious.

I plunged a corn chip into the most delicious salsa I'd ever tasted, rich and not too spicy. "Speaking of where you grew up," I said, "I was looking at some travel brochure pictures of Veracruz. It's beautiful."

She nodded. "Yes, some places are quite beautiful."

"I have been thinking," I said, "about getting away to a place with a beach and palm trees."

"You have beaches with palm trees right here in California," she pointed out.

"Yes, but… surrounded by millions of people breathing down my neck night and day, honking their horns, elbowing me out of the way at the supermarket, scratching my car in parking lots. I need someplace quiet. I need a retreat."

She gave a little shrug. "One small part of my father's land has a beach, but it is not on the ocean. It borders Lake Catemaco."

"Are there palm trees?"

"A few, yes," she said. "And some dates."

I told her my idea of creating a boutique resort where exhausted Americans could come to relax in a peaceful, uncluttered tropical setting and have everything taken care of at a manageable price.

"A few guests at a time," I said. "Specialize in small groups, and then maybe expand into vacation packages. Just the thing for attorneys in stressful circumstances who need to get away and rethink their lives."

"You mean like a corporate conference center?"

"Possibly," I said. "Later on."

Our waiter showed up with drinks and more appetizers. We munched a little in silence. Then she spoke again.

"That takes a lot of capital."

Her statement caught me by surprise. What could she know about what it took to build and run a retreat? Not wanting to be rude, I kept that thought to myself.

She went on, following her train of thought. "Do you have a plan to find money before you start? You will need investors."

"I can find investors," I replied. "That won't be a problem. As for guests, I know a whole lot of attorneys in dire need of a break from their legal practice. Clients always want something they can't have. They expect you to fulfill the most unrealistic demands."

I sighed. "Being an attorney is painfully stressful much of the time. It's mentally, emotionally, and physically fatiguing—always adversarial and combative. It takes a lot out of you. Attorneys need a place to recharge."

She leaned toward me. "So, you also feel that way?"

"Of course," I said. "I'm getting bankrupted by my divorce, living in a tiny one-bedroom apartment, and watching my ex-partner attempt to steal my law practice!"

Amelia sat back with a little smile. It irritated me that she would laugh at me.

"I've never met anyone like you," she said, looking up at me with a sideways smile. "You have so much ability, but you look at the hole in the ground instead of the mountain of treasure sitting next to it in the sunshine."

It took me a moment to digest that. Was I really being that negative? The intensity of her gaze seemed to require a reply. "So why the heck am I paying Dr. Sid all this money, when I can have all the psychoanalysis I need for the cost of buying you a meal?" I asked, as much from awe as from irritation.

She laughed again. "Sorry, I didn't mean to be psychoanalyzing you."

"And anyway," I countered with a smirk, "how do you

know how much ability I have?"

"Oh, I've read about you," she said.

"Read about me? Where?"

"In the newspaper. You're famous."

My eyebrows shot up and I almost choked on the chip I was chewing. "I'm famous?"

"Yes. I read about the way you helped that mother who lost her twin sons in an automobile accident. They were suing her for damages, and you got the case thrown out."

Aaaah. Yes, that one had made the papers. "The boys were at fault," I explained, "and the people in the other vehicle had some injuries. But the poor woman lost both of her sons. She had suffered enough. I just did what was right. That was a 'pro bono,' a no-fee case I was happy to do."

"Well, you see? That is how I know about your potential."

"That's it?"

"No. I also happen to know that you built a law firm that was so successful your partner decided to try to steal it out from under you."

"True." Ooh, this was feeling good.

Our dishes arrived. Amelia was right about the food being incredibly tasty. After a while, as if she was listening to my thoughts, she honed right in again. "How are you doing with Dr. Sid?" she asked. "Has he given you any more goals?"

"Doing great," I said. "And if my goal was to find out why my whole life shattered like a broken window, I have that figured out. One good look in the mirror showed me who was to blame for that.

"First, I married a woman I thought I loved, but who never loved me. Oh, maybe she loved me for a time, but what she really loved was my money, and the things I could give her.

"Second, I brought a partner into my firm who's incompetent as an attorney and a crook, a liar, and a drunk, to boot.

"And now they're both doing their darnedest to get one up on me. I created all this with my bad choices, and now I have become the fly in their webs. That much is clear."

Chomping a potato, I shrugged. "Dr. Sid will fix everything else."

Before she could comment, I said, "Amelia, I climbed the ladder of success only to discover when I got to the top that I'd climbed the wrong ladder."

She shook her head. "You didn't climb the wrong ladder, you got thrown off. There is only one ladder, Sam. You need to get back on it and start climbing up again."

I put my fork down. "Let me explain this to you. What people don't realize is that law school does not teach you how to practice law. It teaches you how to pass the bar exam."

Amelia didn't say anything, just sat there and listened.

"I went to law school because my father had great attorneys who looked out for him and his crazy business schemes. He got tired of paying them all the time, so he told me to become a lawyer because that's where the real money was, the prestige.

"'Look at Martin's car,' he used to say. Allen Martin was his top attorney. 'Guy drives a Cadillac. Wife has a Lincoln.

Big house. Flashy office. Fashionable dresser. That's the way to go.'

"So, that's the way I went. He told me go work for someone and learn how to be an attorney."

The waiter stood by our table again. Amelia spoke to him. He cleared away the empty plates and disappeared back into the kitchen.

"I ordered the flan for us," she said. "Please, go on with your story."

"When you pass the bar exam, you receive a letter from the State Bar of California that starts out, 'We are pleased to inform you that you have successfully passed the California Bar Exam.'

"As I look back to that day, it occurs to me that the letter from the State Bar should have read, 'We regret to inform you....'

"But what did I know? I was elated. I leapt in the air and shouted out loud. This was followed immediately by a cold and terrifying thought: I didn't know how to actually practice law. How was I going to learn?

"I went to see my old law school president. He gave me the number of an attorney, Hugh Benjamin, who had contacted him looking for a new graduate to work as his associate attorney.

"I was excited, thrilled, and panicked, all at the same time. It took me two days to finally call. Mr. Benjamin received me well and thanked me for applying. I told him about my lack of experience, and that I needed some help. He laughed.

'Meet me at my office and we'll do the interview over lunch,' he said.

"I got to his office a half hour early. It was in a beautiful upscale building on Wilshire Boulevard, in West Los Angeles. His name was up there on the door in large gold lettering along with two others, right above ATTORNEYS AT LAW.

"That was impressive. I paced around, hands in my pockets, waiting to go in.

"Then I heard this smooth, confident voice behind me. 'You don't have to rush, Sam,' the voice said. 'You're twenty minutes early.'

"I turned around to receive one of Hugh's irresistible engaging smiles and his firm handshake. 'Call me Huey,' he said. He was very self-assured, with a dry, sardonic humor. 'Let's go eat,' he said. 'I'll drive.'

"I will never forget when we got to the parking structure and he pointed to a shiny brand new black Porsche 911 with a whale tail. He saw my astonishment and lust. 'Get in and pull your seat belt tight,' he grinned.

"At the restaurant, I started to tell Huey about the concerns I was having with regard the practice of law. 'Sam,' he said, 'first things first. What do you want to drink?'

"This was new to me, since I didn't really drink. Even in college, I got drunk at twenty, vomited, and that ended my interest in alcohol. Although I did drink beer. I mean, it was college. But I don't think I ever finished one.

"So I told him, 'I'll have what you have.' Big mistake. Four hours later, we were still sitting at the bar, downing drinks and talking about lawyers and judges, their character and personalities. I don't remember having lunch."

Amelia was listening closely, but now she pointed to my dessert. I dug into the flan and took a bite. "This is incredible," I told her. "It just disappears on your tongue, and leaves the scent of oranges."

She looked pleased. "I'm glad you like it." She took another bite. "So what happened with this Huey?"

"When it was finally time to leave, Huey said to me, 'If you want to learn how to practice law the right way, you should come work for me.' He didn't sound or act like he'd been drinking at all, and he got me back to my car safe and sound.

"'Let me know what you decide,' he said. He waved goodbye and drove off in his gorgeous Porsche. After he was gone, I left my car there and took a taxi home."

Amelia paused with her fork in midair. "So, what did you decide?"

I smiled. "I went to work for Huey, of course."

Amelia rested her arms on the table. "He made a big impact on you. Tell me more about him."

"Huey was raised in San Francisco. His mother was Scottish, married to a Russian immigrant who worked for the federal government. Huey's mother was a cynic, very harsh to his father. His father was quiet, friendly, and always ready to give you a smile.

"His mother served dinner at exactly the same time every day. Her crustiness exhausted Huey's emotional bond with her, so much so that when she died in her late eighties he showed up at her funeral more out of a sense of obligation than out of any real sense of loss.

"Huey began drinking early in his college days and never looked back. He had a muscular body with thick arms and legs, and spent a lot of time lifting weights. He played handball and tennis almost daily, and loved snow skiing in Lake Tahoe.

"Once in law school, the dean told him his class standing was number three from the bottom of his class. Huey didn't care. He was still going to graduate from law school.

"Class standing and social class meant nothing to him. He just wanted to get through law school, pass the bar exam, and make enough money to pay for his life style."

Amelia's brow wrinkled. "He sounds more like a country club golf buddy. How did you learn about the law?"

I had to smile. "I'll tell you a story," I said, "the beginning of my real world education. A month or so after I joined Huey's office, I was trying to file documents with the Court Clerk on a divorce case.

"I had just gotten a second Notice of Rejection and was in the Clerk's office talking to them when Huey came in. The clerk's whole demeanor changed, from stern taskmaster to kindly librarian.

"'Evelyn!' Huey said brightly, giving her his thousand-watt smile. 'How's it going today?'" I role-played this for Amelia, stretching my arms out wide, just the way Huey had.

"She warmed up immediately. 'Hello, Huey,' Evelyn said.

"'Evelyn, this gentleman is my associate, Sam Weisman.' He glanced down at the Clerk's Notice of Rejection. 'Evelyn, is there a problem with his papers?' he asked, all innocence.

"'He's missing a few things,' she said.

"'Sure,' Huey said, piling on the charm. 'What does he need to do?'

"She paused one moment, then said, 'These two boxes need to be checked, right here.'

"Nodding, Huey said, 'Do you have a pen?' She smiled and said, 'I'll just check it for you.'

"'Thanks, Evelyn,' Huey said with a wink. 'And keep an eye on my associate here.'

"She smiled back, and we stepped aside. The next attorney in line handed Evelyn his document. She looked it over. Her face took on a stern expression, like frost covering a window, and she stamped REJECTED on the form and handed it back.

"Irritated, he said, 'You people are unbelievable! Now, what's the problem?' Evelyn told him, 'You have two boxes without the correct check marks. Fix it and bring it back.'

"The lawyer stormed off in a huff. Huey watched him leave and turned to me. 'The moral?' he whispered. 'Be especially nice to the clerks.'

"I've never had Huey's charm or confidence, but he showed me how the smart guys do it. Huey took personal pride in shaping me, in teaching me.

"It was like when I was a child and rode with my father in his car to and from his tailor shop. I would listen to Huey's views on everything, whether we were in a restaurant bar or sitting in the courthouse waiting for our cases to be assigned to a judge.

"Despite his easygoing nature, Huey didn't trust anyone or anything. He particularly disliked arrogance and bullying. So do I.

"And that's a big part of why I'm having such a hard time with my ex-wife and my ex-partner. They're both arrogant bullies. They constantly amaze me. I just can't believe anyone would do the things they do.

"You see, I came from an innocent suburban background, insulated from the tough streets and bad neighborhoods of Los Angeles. I thought everyone was a good person, and that when people spoke it was with sincerity and accuracy.

"Foolish, naive me. I confused the look of physical maturity in people's faces with wisdom. I awoke happy every morning ready for a new day of adventure. That was what Huey liked about me, my freshness, my enjoyment of each day, my easy laugh, that I wasn't hypercritical and jaded about life."

I fell silent, reflecting. "Now that easy laugh is gone," I said. It was the first time that realization had hit me. "And I miss it."

Amelia sat forward. "You sound like a tragic love song!" She smiled and squeezed my hand.

"As long as the song doesn't end with the man getting hanged or jumping off a bridge," I said.

"How long were you with Huey?" she asked.

"I worked with him for about two years," I told her, "and

then I opened my own law office. Huey wasn't the least upset. Just the opposite; he was actually happy for me. 'Well, Sam, you're on your way,' he told me."

Amelia turned to our waiter and asked for the bill. "*La cuenta*, por favor." Some Spanish I finally understood. I pulled out my wallet.

"No, no." She held up her hand. "It is my turn."

"Amelia..."

"My treat," she interrupted, and with finality laid some cash on the waiter's tray.

I felt uncomfortable. As if she could read my mind, she said, "Sam, don't feel guilty. It's all right." She looked up. "Oh, good, here is someone I want you to meet."

A little round dark man with a full Pancho Villa moustache stepped up to the table. I stood up to greet him, startled to see that he was Amelia's height. He looked like one of those giant Olmec face stones dressed in chef's whites.

"Sam," she said, "this is Chef Rolando, also from Veracruz." She nodded in my direction. "Sam Weisman."

He beamed and nodded several times, sticking out his hand to shake. I expected him to say something in Spanish.

"Pleased to meet you, Mr. Weisman," he said in perfect English. "Friends of Amelia's are always welcome here."

"Rolando is an old family friend," Amelia said, patting his shoulder. "He and my uncle grew up together."

I mumbled something about how much I had enjoyed the meal. We shook hands again, and Amelia and I stood up to leave.

My jaw dropped when we arrived at her car. "You drive a new Lexus LS?"

"I lease them every two years," she said and beeped the door open. "It's a nice car, and comfortable for clients."

I didn't know what to say. She turned around at that moment, and suddenly we were cheek to cheek. I could feel her breath coming in short gasps. She leaned back against the car and her arms went around my neck.

The best things in life are free- But you can keep them for the birds and bees- Now give me money (that's what I want)!

"I don't believe it!" I shouted as our bodies pulled apart from each other, the moment gone.

She was laughing. "You left your phone on," she said as I grabbed the phone and shut it off. "You're not going to answer him?"

"I'll call him back later," I said. "I grew up in a house without alcohol or cigarettes. Instead, we had anxiety and neurosis. But my father doesn't have heart disease or ulcers. He's a carrier—he transfers heart disease and ulcers to other people."

"Do you know why he called?"

"Actually, I do," I said. "I have to represent him in an arbitration hearing tomorrow."

"Oh," she said, "that sounds interesting."

"Not really. It's going to be another train wreck I won't get paid for."

"Sam," she said. "Stop looking at the hole in the ground."

She got into her Lexus and drove away.

11

A man who is "of sound mind"
is one who keeps the inner madman
under lock and key.

—*Paul Valery,*
Mauvaises pensées et autres, 1942

I was in the offices of an upscale law firm, standing at a urinal in the men's room. My father's arbitration was being held in their large conference room.

I had barely made it to the restroom and was feeling a huge sense of relief. My briefcase sat at my feet, next to a box containing all the relevant folders, files, documents, maps, notes, and restaurant napkins with miscellaneous scribblings.

I was trying to organize my thoughts. I wanted to be fresh, crisp, and ready to argue my father's case.

My phone rang, its normal ring, and I scrambled to grab it. I opened it up with one hand, but it slipped away and fell into the urinal, right in line with the stream of pee.

Oh, no! I didn't know who had called, and now my phone was likely ruined. What else could go wrong?

"Sam!" My father's voice came scratchy and distant from some unknown location in the building. "Sam! It's your father.

Where are you?"

I did the urinal man dance, trying to zip up my pants with one hand and grab my phone out of the urinal with the other.

"Sam, answer me! People are waiting here."

I shook the phone and held it up near my ear, not wanting to touch it to my skin. No sound. No time to clean it up. Dismayed, I closed the phone and dropped it into my pants pocket.

"SAM!" He was shouting now. "Can you hear me?"

I hurried to answer to my father's impatient cry.

"Dad!"

"Where are you?"

"I'll be right there." I picked up my briefcase and the box of files and other paraphernalia and hurried out.

The lobby was beautiful. This was a major downtown law firm with stunning décor. I went into the waiting room, where my father sat at the end of a row of chairs, talking on his cell phone.

"My son just came in," he said. "I'll call you back." To me, he said, "Partners. They'll be here soon."

I put my stuff on a chair and sat down to wait for them to call us into the conference room. On the chair next to me sat a shiny stack of classy looking spiral-bound booklets with 'El Camino Estates,' the name of my father's real estate development firm, on the front.

"What's this?" I asked him.

"Oh, Diane did those a few months ago."

I flipped through the booklet. It was a first class financial analysis of the project. I could see why he'd been able to interest investors in the project. This made it look like you couldn't lose.

"Why didn't you show me this before?" I asked him.

He waved me off. "It was in the car. I gave you all the important stuff." His cell rang and he turned away, talking with a serious business tone into the phone.

Speak of the devil. The door opened and Diane walked in, looking sharp in a beautifully tailored business suit. She sat down with the booklets on the chair between us.

"You ready to take up the sword for Dad again?" she asked, grinning.

I held up the booklet. "You did this?"

"Yeah," she said. "That's how Dad sold the project to the investors. 'My daughter, the financial genius.' You know how he is. Why?"

"Did he pay you for it?"

She exhaled sharply, the corners of her lips turning up in a tight little smile. "You know better than that."

"This is a very expensive professional prospectus," I said. "Why would you do that?"

Diane turned to look right at me, faintly amused or curious, I wasn't sure which. "I call it the law of indirect reward," she said. "You do something for someone for nothing. Then, later on, something comes your way that pays you back."

I didn't know what she was talking about. "Like what?"

"Okay," she said. "Dad calls me up, 'Diane, how can I make money on this deal?' So I gather up all his incredibly complicated plans, partnership documents, criss-crossing contracts and wacko ideas, and distill them down into a business plan with detailed costs and expenses and a projected potential return on investment.

"But, instead of invoicing him, I take a small percentage interest in the project. He gets whatever analysis or projections I can give him and I don't have to listen to him squawk about having to pay me."

"You do all that for him for free?" I couldn't believe this. "You let him work you."

Diane shrugged. "I've done it for years. A kind of silent investor. Actually it's paid off pretty well."

"I don't believe you. You can't make money that way!"

Diane sat up. "I've got seven hundred thousand dollars that says different."

I felt like I'd been slugged. I didn't know what to say. How could this possibly be true?

Diane stood up, glancing at her watch. "Look, I've got a meeting," she said. "Tell Dad to call me if he needs anything explained, or whatever." She paused a moment. "Go get 'em, St. George." And she walked out.

I felt like I was in a pressure cooker on high heat with no safety valve. I could not believe Diane had made that kind of money, and I'd gotten nothing.

Over the years I figured I had made maybe three or four thousand dollars defending Dad countless times. I had no idea my sister had been working with him like that. Why hadn't anyone told me?

Just then the secretary opened the door and motioned for us to come into the conference room. I grabbed my things and got my father off the phone, and we went in to take our seats at the long table.

At the head of the table sat an urbane, distinguished looking man who would be our arbitrator. I had met him once at some law seminar or State Bar function.

"Good morning," he said. "My name is W. Miles Chase. I'm the senior partner of this law firm. We specialize in real estate transactions and were selected as arbitrator for this case. The arbitration is going to be informal, so please call me Bill."

He loosened his tie and unbuttoned his collar button. "But my decision will have the same force and effect as any court judgment. I will make my decision based on the testimony and evidence I receive.

"Mind you, this is a binding arbitration, meaning that my decision is final on all issues, and without possibility of appeal."

My father was already bored and looking around.

"Please know," Chase continued, "that I have received and read each of the parties' briefs and have reviewed all of the documents submitted in support.

"What I want to hear now is your story, and I want to hear it out of your own mouth. Therefore, we will dispense with opening statements by the attorneys. Since no one requested it, we have no court reporter present to record the proceedings."

I glanced across at the other side. Riley Smythe was representing the investors. Smythe, with a "y" and an "e." We'd been adversaries several times in other court cases.

"Now, you attorneys, when you object, please understand that the evidentiary rules in this arbitration will be relaxed compared to the rules of evidence in a court trial."

Smythe looked up. "How will we know the rules?"

Chase smiled again. "When you make your objection, I'll let you know. I want the parties to feel they've had their day in court."

I could only hope my father hadn't withheld anything critical to the case that I knew nothing about.

Mr. Chase explained that the plaintiffs would tell their story first, and why they were mad at Benjamin Weisman.

Smythe said his only witnesses were the investors, who just wanted their money back.

For the defense, the only expert witness was to be Diane Weisman. However, since she could not be physically present, her presence would be known through the project prospectus which she had authored and which the defendant had used to promote his project.

"Mr. Smythe," Chase said, "you have fifteen investors here. Can just one of them tell the story?"

Smythe introduced one of his clients, who explained they were suing my father, as general partner, for fraud. They wanted their investment back, plus interest and their attorney's fees.

In a nutshell, he told the arbitrator, they had discovered they couldn't build houses where originally planned and had concluded that my father was pulling a fast one that would net him his fee even as the investors lost their investment.

When he was done, Mr. Chase turned to my father. "Now I would like to hear from the defendant. Mr. Weisman, are you ready?"

"Sure," said my father.

I turned cold in my seat. In all my father's other cases, I had spoken for him. Was he going to blare on like he had at the coffee shop, to the point of utter confusion?

"Just tell us your side, in your own words," Chase prompted.

"Well, Bill, here's what happened."

I leapt to my feet. "I object!" There was dead silence in the room.

Chase turned to me. "What's your objection?"

"I don't know of a legal basis for my objection, and I don't know what he's going tell you," I said.

Chase looked at me closely. "You can't object to what your own client is going to say."

My mouth was getting dry. "Can't you just accept the information in the brief, in lieu of my father's testimony?"

Chase was frowning now. "No," he said. "And, you're the wrong attorney to object. If there is an objection, it should be Mr. Smythe making it." He turned to Smythe. "Do you have an objection?"

Smythe was doing his best not to grin. "No, of course not," he said. "I want to hear this, too."

"I think we all do," Chase said. He turned back to my

father. "Mr. Weisman, do you want to testify?"

My father looked at me and I looked at him. To his credit, my father said, "No, I think I'll just let my son handle this."

I grabbed my copy and held up the brief. "We submit the information in the arbitration brief as our evidence for your consideration."

"Very well," Chase said, and turned back to Smythe. "Mr. Smythe, you may now make your closing statement."

Smythe turned the arbitration into bad daytime television, courtroom antics of the first order.

To make him look guilty and liable from the beginning, he never referred to my father as Benjamin Weisman, but only as "the defendant." He accused my father of all types of fraud, lies, and misrepresentations.

From the beginning, Smythe claimed, my father had known that this was a project that could never succeed.

He maintained that my father had designed the project merely to obtain Smythe's clients' money, solely to enrich himself. And that in fact the project had never proceeded beyond the blueprint stage.

My father leaned over and whispered to me. "After the flood, we just flipped the drawings over. The houses are still going in, but down at the southeastern end."

Chase was trying to get my attention, "Attorney Weisman?"

I stood up. "Your Honor, please refer to the documents submitted with the arbitration brief for the defense, which Mr. Smythe failed to mention.

"Exhibit 3 is a map revised after the flood, a map that has been inspected, reviewed, and approved by the San Diego County Planning Department, and which bears their stamp of approval.

"This document shows that Ben Weisman has not only done everything he promised for the investors to this point, but also that he is prepared to begin construction immediately based on the new approved plans."

I felt like the king of high-risk response. I glanced over at Smythe.

"Weisman," Smythe said, "you've got an attitude."

"I've got a lot of attitudes," I quipped. "Which attitude are you referring to?"

Mr. Chase spoke sternly. "Counsel, please refrain from personal sniping." He turned to me. "Continue, Mr. Weisman."

"My father," I went on, "did not deceive or mislead anyone. 'Riparian' simply means the interface between land and a river or stream, or adjacent to a flowing stream or river water.

"Because the property still borders on flowing water, by switching the location of the houses my father has actually protected the investors' investment. He did not commit fraud, and is not liable.

"In fact," I went on, "he is fully ready and willing to build all twenty home sites immediately at the other end of the development. And he is also prepared to construct the green belt area that enhances the value of the development.

"These are premier waterfront or near-waterfront home

sites in an exclusive area. The value will not be damaged or affected in any way by relocating the home sites. This real estate investment will return a substantial profit to the investors."

I sat down. There wasn't a sound in the room.

Mr. Chase looked thoughtful and shuffled some papers.

"Well," he said finally, "this doesn't take a lot of cogitation. I am ruling in favor of Mr. Weisman, based on the original contract, as adjusted with the approval of the San Diego County Planning Department. Plaintiff's request for court costs and attorney fees is denied."

The investors were huddled around Smythe. Chase pointed his pencil at them. "You investors, pay attention," he said. "Mr. Weisman has a terrific project here. I know his partners listed in Exhibit 4. They are first class land development real estate brokers, attorneys, and accountants. Mr. Weisman's firm has worked with them on several occasions.

"And Mr. Weisman's business approach of pre-selling enough homes to pay for the development loan is a proven sound practice. This is one deal I wish I had invested in. Mr. Weisman is going to make you all a lot of money."

After that, the ice broke. My father and the investors shook hands and talked to each other like nothing was ever wrong. I put my things back in my briefcase, amazed once again at how gracious and pleasant he could be with near strangers.

Oddly, I still felt used.

My father came over to me. "My partners are here," he said. "I've got to go. I have an appointment with some investors on another real estate deal."

I shot him a cross look. "What about my fee?"

He smiled. "How many times have I told you, 'Don't work for pennies, go for the bucks'?"

"You said the partners would take care of me."

As he walked away, he said, "And call Alfonso. It's right up your alley."

"I can't," I said. "I dropped my phone." I didn't tell him where I'd dropped it.

"So get another one."

I was about to retort that he owed me a cell phone, that if I hadn't been trying to juggle his legal mess I wouldn't have dropped it, but Carl Victor, one of my father's partners, came up to me with an envelope. He thanked me and shook my hand. I opened the envelope.

It contained a check from the partnership for $5,000. Finally.

"Hey, Dad!" I called out. He looked over his shoulder. I held up the check.

"See?" he said. "I told you you'd get paid, and you did." Just like that, he and his partners were gone.

On my way home I stopped at the phone store and bought a new phone.

Later, I sat on a chaise lounge by the pool in my swim trunks, feeling the warm sun smooth out the kinks and wrinkles from the morning.

I smelled of tanning lotion and pool chemicals, and the sunblock stung my eyes, but the kids were over for a visit and that made it fun. Diane had picked them up while I was at the arbitration and brought them over for an afternoon by the pool.

Rachel sat in a chair next to me, watching Ryan do cannonballs off the deck into the pool. Adam lay nearby on his towel, soaking up the sun. He was getting really dark this summer.

"I won a court case for your grandfather today," I said to Rachel.

"That's great, Dad," she said with a proud smile, a lovely smile. I was glad she had inherited the best of Cindy's genes. I just hoped she had inherited the best of mine, if there were any.

Ryan came dripping up to us and plopped down on the concrete like a sack of water balloons.

"Move off, wet boy!" Adam barked, turning away on his towel. "You're worse than a dog after a bath."

Ryan made a gnarly face at Adam's back. "Your face is going to freeze like that," Adam said, casting a deprecating look over his shoulder. "We'll have to stick you in the garden like a gnome."

Ryan turned to me, as if worried about his face.

"Hey," I said to him, "how's your asthma?"

"Mom got me some medicine," he said, rubbing his nose. "It's better now. I just don't understand those cats. You can't even pet them or play with them. They snarl and hiss and then they claw you and run away. They're no fun."

Adam did a sudden roll over. "Hey, Aunt Diane, you have

any more of those skateboard T-shirts, like in black?"

"You would like them, you punk," Diane said, grinning. "How's that new Brokenbones skateboard? I hear they're carbon fiber with state-of-the-art wheel trucks."

"Best board I ever rode," Adam declared.

I sat up. "You gave him a skateboard?"

"By the way, thanks for the furniture, Dad," Rachel said quietly.

"Oh, good," I said, "it was delivered then. How do you like it?"

She twirled the towel between her fingers. "I mean, I'm really glad not to have to sleep on the floor. But… it's just not my style. It's too froufrou. You know, like the kind of stuff Mom would buy for herself."

"Bad daddy," Adam said.

"What do you want me to do?" I asked her.

"Can you take it back and let me pick out my own?"

"I'll have to check into the return policy," I said. "I'll call them and see." I made yet another mental note.

She smiled. "Thanks, Dad."

Adam rolled over. "Beware the furniture movers."

Late that night I sat in my tiny kitchenette eating Chinese takeout, reflecting back on the events of the day. In the end, the arbitration had gone well. I had come out a hero. And I'd been paid. So why didn't I feel more exultant?

Getting paid was good. At least I could relax a little around the financial issue. I should call Roxann about the disability policy in the morning. That made me think of Johnny Redman. I had just seen a piece about him in a sports magazine, something about him still coming in last place but qualifying for the PGA tour.

Through the steaming fog surrounding the spa, barely illuminated by tiny blue lights, the dark angel floated by like a shadow scented with exotic body lotion. Silently she slipped out of her robe and into the bubbling spa.

I held my breath. She was wearing nothing at all, except a fancy spiked stick barrette that held her black hair up off her neck. I couldn't see through the steaming fog, only a glimpse as she slid into the churning warm water.

She seemed completely comfortable.

I was tired, relaxed, and completely curious. "What's that aroma?" I asked.

Her eyes stayed closed, head back. "European Body Indulgence." Her voice was low and firm. "I rub it all over my body. Do you like it?"

"It smells very…" My voice tailed off as I searched for the word. "Very European," I finally managed.

"Europe interests me," she said. "We're studying Friedrich Nietzsche in my philosophy class. You know, that 19th-century German writer who thought God was dead?"

"Yes, yes," I said quickly, "Nietzsche."

"He wanted to question all doctrines that drain life's expansive energies," she said, "regardless of whether the society at large embraced them or not."

She opened her eyes and looked at me with cold laser

beams. "He believed in the Ubermensch, the higher person who can seize power by the force of their will."

"Oh, yes," I said quickly. I had never been intellectual, but at that moment I was ready and willing to convert.

Still fixing me with her look, she stood up in the roiling steam, water running down her torso, and raised her arms over her head to adjust her barrette.

I was entranced, but strangely detached. Maybe I was growing up. Sitting there admiring her lovely breasts, I flashed on the 'No Nude Swimming' sign. She wasn't swimming, I rationalized. She was sitting.

The thought of the 'No Nude Swimming' sign turned my thoughts to Amelia.

12

He who trims himself to suit everyone
will soon whittle himself away.
—*Raymond Hull*

The next morning I woke up rubbing my eyes, wondering whether my little spa experience had actually happened. Or had I dreamed it?

A hot shower brought clarity. She had spoken to me about Nietzsche. *Nietzcshe!* Of all things. Who would have thought her mind would run in such deep waters?

It must have been real. My mind would never have made that up.

After an excellent breakfast of fresh ground coffee, half an orange, and toast with apricot jam, I found my yellow pad and a pen and punched up Roxann's number at Gotcherbach Insurance Services into my cell phone.

I had endured all the physical and psychological exams, filled out all the forms, jumped through all their hoops, done everything they required. But I had yet to see my first disability check.

I let the phone ring once, and then hung up when it struck me that my top priority should be a call to Johnny

Redman's office.

I had done him a number of legal favors in the past, from which he had derived considerable financial benefit. Maybe he would want to invest in a Mexican resort.

A liquid feminine voice answered. "The Redman Partnership Group, how may I help you?" She said her name was Celeste, and that Mr. Redman was out of the office.

I introduced myself as an attorney who had counseled Mr. Redman in the past, and told her I had a lucrative real estate development investment opportunity for him.

She said she would give him the message. I hung up, wondering whether Johnny used the same receptionist employment agency as Dr. Sid.

I punched up Roxann's office again. When she came on the line I explained that I had been expecting a check by now.

"Didn't you get my letter?" she asked dryly.

"What letter?"

"Well, Mr. Weisman..." She sounded tired. "The substance of your employment disability claim was that, due to the debilitating mental stress of your occupation, you were rendered completely emotionally unfit and unable to engage in the daily pursuit of your legal profession.

"However," she droned on, "our investigator found evidence that you have continued to, and are fully capable of, practicing law, with no apparent mentally disabling effects whatsoever."

I fought to control my anger. "Who told you I'm still practicing law?" I asked, keeping my voice even. "Was it

James Watkins? Don't believe him. He's the one who caused my mental disability in the first place." I took a breath. "What exactly did he say?"

"I'm sorry, Mr. Weisman," she said. "I'm not at liberty to divulge our sources or present any proof at this time. Suffice it to say, we have rejected your claim based on your ongoing practice of law.

"When you can provide a doctor's letter stating that you are mentally unfit and emotionally unable to practice law, we will be happy to review your application. Have a nice day."

I knew Dr. Sid would give me such a letter. He was the one who had suggested filing a disability claim, after all. I made a mental note to ask him about it.

In spite of my stellar handling of my dad's case, my nerves felt like thin little wires that would break at the slightest jangle. But she did have a point. I had been practicing law.

I snapped the phone shut, shaking with frustration. It was going to take time to build up a new client base, and James had locked me out of all my old clients with the partnership lawsuit.

Until I could get a letter from Sid, I was going to have to figure out some way to keep the cash flow coming in to pay my expenses, Cindy's expenses, child support, and everything else.

The phone rang. I ignored it, still stewing about Roxann's complete lack of concern for my situation. But the ring kept on going, and I couldn't stand it. I opened the phone.

"Hey, Sam," said the familiar cheery voice. "Alfonso Lechuga! Glad I caught you."

My heart sank. “Hello, Alfonso,” I said. “I’m glad to hear from you, too, but I’m right in the middle of drafting a partnership agreement for a doctor and it has to be ready for our eleven o’clock meeting.”

“Oh, no problem,” he said. This guy was nothing if not patient. And persistent. “You’re a very busy man. Ben told me you did a great job for him at the arbitration hearing.”

It would have been nice to hear that direct from my father.

“Can I get back to you later?” I suggested.

“Of course,” Alfonso said. “Call me when you get a chance and I will tell you about the job I have for you.”

“Thank you, Alfonso,” I said. Where did he get all this joviality? I hung up.

Flipping through my files, I dug out a blank partnership agreement, an open generic agreement with lots of blanks to fill in. No reason to draft anything extensive. This was for Dr. Sid, after all.

Seeing the word ‘partnership’ did give me a twinge, reminding me of the looming Meet and Confer with James and that smug yuppie, arrogant, golf-playing attorney of his. “Both of them should keep their arrogance behind their zippers where it belongs.”

We were going to have to come up with a report to give to Judge Flores in about ten days. Facing them would be aggravating enough, but what shook me was the thought that I could actually lose that case. It would ruin me. I could not imagine anything worse.

The phone rang. I answered quickly, hoping to hear Amelia's voice on the other end.

"Hi!" a voice said. "This is Chris Warren from Vinnie's Vinyl Siding. Have we got a deal for you, Mr. Weisman! Top shelf vinyl siding installed cheap. A quality product and quality service."

Chris rattled on about the lowest price, installation in half the time the competition took, and how wonderful the finished product would look, as well as offering excellent protection from the elements for years to come.

In the politest tone I could muster I said, "Chris, excuse me for interrupting. I am very interested in your product and I would love to learn more. But I am really busy at the moment. Give me your home phone number and I'll call you tonight. Believe me, I want to hear all about the deal you're offering."

That stunned him. He didn't know what to do. On my end, it was all I could do to keep from guffawing out loud. But I waited for him to recover.

"I'm not going to give you my home number," he said at last.

"All right, your cell number, then."

Peeved, Chris said, "I'm not giving you my cell number! You could call me at all hours of the day and night and harass me till I had to change the number!"

I slipped an imaginary dagger out from its sheath. "What do you think you're doing to me, Chris? You call me at my home, over and over. Did I give you permission to call me? No! I've deleted six of your messages this week alone."

"I'm just trying to get you a deal!" he whined.

"You're harassing me."

"Look," he said, not ready to give up yet. "I've got a terrific product that can beautify and protect your house, and save you money. You really shouldn't pass this up, Mr. W. Your wife will be happy and proud."

It was time to use the imaginary dagger to pluck his eyes from their sockets. "Chris," I thundered, "I'm in the middle of an evil divorce from the devil's own spawn. She took my house, my business, and my life. I live in a one-bedroom apartment. What possible use could I have for vinyl siding?"

"Well, if that's the case, why did you answer the phone?" And Chris hung up.

I almost hurled my cell phone onto the floor. What stopped me, besides realizing how much it would cost to replace it again, was staring at the thick carpet under the table.

The phone would never shatter with a satisfying explosion of broken pieces flying around the room. It would probably bounce and then plop down six feet away, inoperable but whole. Staring at me. Dead, but not destroyed.

I shoved the partnership agreement into a file folder and headed out to Dr. Sid's office.

His parking lot was filled with people bustling back and forth and curious bystanders milling around. A TV remote broadcast truck was parked sideways in front of the entrance to the building.

I had to drive to the far end for a parking space, and then walk all the way back to his office. What in the world could be going on? I hoped it was nothing bad. I didn't see any police or emergency vehicles, so I guessed it was all right.

As I approached the entrance, a blonde woman in her thirties came whirling past wearing a pale green T-shirt that read:

Luck is when preparation
meets opportunity.

That stopped me. I turned around to watch her walk to her car. On the back it read:

I make my own luck.

Astounded, I headed up to the front door amidst a flurry of pastel T-shirts. One pink shirt gave me a clue:

I'm bi-chotic – I want it both ways.

On the back it said:

You can't eat your cake and have it too.

I was almost afraid to go inside.

Dr. Sid's receptionist, looking eye-catching in a yellow T-shirt, saw me and waved me toward his office. The front of her shirt proclaimed:

Success is inevitable if you don't give up.

She saw me looking and turned to show me the back:

I give up – I give in.

I pushed through the crowd down to Dr. Sid's waiting room.

A short, determined woman in her fifties came striding up the hallway carrying what looked like a fancy designer bag from Nordstrom's, only it said

Sid the Psych

under a drawing of a grinning Dr. Sid pointing to a large block letters that said:

Dr. Sid's Salon –
We make you feel good…
and look good.

Right behind her, waving goodbye, was the real Dr. Sid.

"Remember, Dorothy," he called after her. "Does it really matter?"

Dorothy waved back. "Thank you for the shirts," she called back over her shoulder.

I could not imagine what was going on.

"Sam!" Dr. Sid called to me with excitement. "Come in, come in! I can't wait to show you what we've done!"

Under his suit coat, Dr. Sid was wearing a light blue

T-shirt. I couldn't make out the words on it.

I followed him into the waiting room but stopped short when I saw the huge group of people gathered there. On the wall was a giant corkboard plastered with pastel T-shirts sporting contradictory sayings.

The receptionist was on her feet, selling T-shirts like crazy, swiping credit cards through the checkout machine and bagging the sold shirts.

In the Post Office, people complained about waiting in line. At Dr. Sid's office they were calm, cheerful, and waiting patiently to part with their money.

Dr. Sid was about to say something to me when a local TV news crew came over to interview him. I recognized the reporter, Mirela somebody.

Dr. Sid joked with her, beaming and pointing to the wall and then at the crowd. He gestured for me to join him.

"Here's the man," Dr. Sid told the TV crew. "Sam, come on over."

"They're not going to interview me, are they?"

Dr. Sid gave me the double eyebrow shuffle. "I'm the new Armani!" he grinned. "Look!" He pointed to a shopping bag. "I even have a logo. Nice, huh?"

Dr. Sid explained to the TV crew that he was expanding into the next office to build a boutique he would call Dr. Sid's Salon. He pointed to the blueprints on his desk.

The construction workers had hung sheet plastic over the wall they had already started knocking out. The sound of their hammering and power drills was practically inaudible, though, over the noise of the crowd.

Dr. Sid walked back over to where I stood, agape at the goings-on. "You brought the agreement, right?" he asked.

"Yes," I said, holding up the folder. "I have it here."

"One of my patients owns The Party Shop, the high-end T-shirt company downtown. That's why I want the rights to sell the T-shirts."

As he turned to ask the TV interviewer whether she had everything she needed, it crossed my mind that The Party Shop was Diane's client, too.

Mirela, the TV reporter, asked whether I was going to make a statement.

"I don't know what to say," I shrugged.

Dr. Sid stepped right in, putting his arm around me for the camera. "If it weren't for Sam Weisman," he said, "there would be no Dr. Sid's Salon."

Clapping me on the shoulder, he whispered in my ear, "Just smile into the camera." Then, looking straight into the camera, he went on like a seasoned actor.

When it was all over he turned back to me. "Follow me, Sam. Let's go into my office."

Finally, it was quiet. I sank deep into the leather chair, drinking herbal tea in the comforting silence. Dr. Sid was behind his desk with a pen in his hand, scribbling on the agreement, drinking coffee from a Dr. Sid's Salon coffee cup as he filled in the blank spaces.

"Dr. Sid, I have a problem only you can resolve," I said.

He looked up. "Oh. Really. And what problem would that

be?" He returned to his scribbles, and I told him what Roxann had said about needing a letter from a doctor saying I was incapable of practicing law."

That got his attention. "Hmm... your defense of your father was a stroke of genius. But it's your overall mental and emotional state I'm concerned about. It makes you unpredictable. You can't practice law if you can't count on your ability to control your emotions. Remind me at the end of the session and I'll have my receptionist draw up a letter for you."

"There's another thing," I said. "I have a new client, other than my dad. This guy was involved in an accident the day James dropped his bombshell on me, right outside our office, and he wants me to represent him."

"So? Do you really think you're fit to take that on right now, Sam?" In his eyes I sensed amusement tempered with compassion.

I heard myself erupt in an exasperated laugh. "God no. I don't know whether I'm coming or going. My whole world is going round in circles."

"Good answer. Let it go for now."

"I will. You're right. Thanks. I'll get him someone else."

He tapped his pen on the contract on his desk. "Should I have an attorney review this and advise me about the terms and conditions to protect my part of the partnership?"

"Most people would have an attorney review an agreement as important as this," I told him.

"Well, you're here. What do you think about this agreement? Is it all right?"

I sat up in the chair. "First of all, we've already agreed I'm unfit to practice law right now. And besides, I'm a party to the agreement! I wrote it. Of course I think it's all right."

Dr. Sid looked at me closely. "Are you sure?"

"Sure? I'm sure for me, but like I said, I'm a party to the agreement. You might consider having a different attorney look it over for you."

Dr. Sid rose from his chair with a dismissive wave of the hand and walked around to me. He leaned back against the front of his desk and folded his arms.

"No, I'll trust you, Sam," he said. "I choose you as my attorney, off the record. I'm still going to charge you for this session, you know."

"What?" I objected. "Why do I have to pay for a session?" He was behaving very strangely, I thought. "I should be charging you for the agreement, plus legal fees for being your attorney."

"It's your investment into the partnership," he said. "What do you think?"

I didn't know what to think. "As your partner, I think the agreement's fine. As your attorney, off the record, I think the agreement's fine."

"Have you read it carefully?"

I shrugged. "I put in the usual stuff."

Dr. Sid peered at me. "So you didn't really give this agreement much attention?"

He seemed irritated. Impatient, even. "You're not taking this business seriously, Sam. You don't seem to understand that this partnership between us could be the proverbial golden goose."

By now I was feeling a bit exasperated. "Look, Dr. Sid, this is our agreement," I said, indicating the paper on his desk. "Just add what you want in it, delete what you want out of it, and I'll sign it."

Dr. Sid stared directly at me, frowning. "If it can go wrong, it will go wrong," he said slowly, with deliberate emphasis.

Then he stood up and pointed his finger at my chest. "Negotiation means, you tell me what you want in the agreement and what you don't want. I tell you what I want in and what I don't want. Then we come to a mutual understanding as to what terms we will both accept."

Why was Dr. Sid lecturing me on how to negotiate? I had written up hundreds of agreements like this one.

Dr. Sid went on, "When you tell me to just insert what I want and you'll sign it, you could lose control of your interest in the agreement."

Dr. Sid stepped over to the coat rack in the corner and hung his jacket on a hook. When he turned back to face me, I could read the T-shirt that had been hidden by his suit coat:

The truth shall set you free.

He turned around to show me the back:

But first, it will make you miserable.

I shook my head. "I've lost control of everything I've ever had!" I said suddenly, blurting it out like a confession.

"You gave it away," said Dr. Sid sharply. "We call that 'fear of responsibility.' When you represent someone else, you're a fiery, indomitable force. When you represent yourself, you cave in too early and give away what you actually need.

"You sabotage your own interests, thinking you're 'trusting' the other party. In reality, you're ducking responsibility. That way, if anything goes wrong, you can believe it wasn't your fault."

I was totally exasperated. "So what do you want me to do?"

"I want you to protect yourself the same way you protect your clients."

"Well," I asked with indignation, "how do I do that?"

Dr. Sid flashed me a warm smile. "Finish this agreement, putting as much attention on it as you would for one of your clients. Then smile, feel good, and be happy. That's your goal."

"Look at my life," I said. "That's not possible."

Dr. Sid slammed his fist into his palm. "That's exactly the point! Let's NOT look at your life. Instead, let's look at how you are going to behave from now on."

Feeling like I'd lost the power of speech, I stood there gaping at him.

Dr. Sid reached over to his side table and handed me a health food cookie. With a grin, he said, "Need milk?"

It was hard to smile while I was chewing.

He stuck out his hand to shake. "Put it there, partner."

"What about the agreement?" I asked.

Still shaking my hand, Dr. Sid said, "This is our agreement. Fifty-fifty."

"So that's it?" I said. "After all that? A handshake?"

"To be confirmed later by written agreement." Dr. Sid beamed like the Dalai Lama. "Written agreements are easier to read." He sat down in the chair opposite me. "So, what else has been going on with you lately?"

I went blank. And then, almost embarrassed, I told him about the pool incident with the dark angel. Dr. Sid listened intently. "So, what happened?"

"Nothing."

"What do you mean, nothing? Come on, tell me what happened. I'm your therapist. This is confidential. Come on, now."

"Well, she's young, beautiful face, firm figure. The perfect twenty-year-old, looks as pretty as she'll ever look in her life. And she was in the spa with me at two in the morning."

"Oh? What happened next?"

Dr. Sid dragged the whole story out of me, a little at a time.

Finally I said, "And she was naked."

"So? What happened?"

"Nothing happened. I sat there admiring all of her toned moving parts, and I realized that was all I wanted. I started thinking about Amelia."

"Aha!" Dr. Sid leaped up. "Amelia! Good boy. Number one, your dark angel is way too young and firm for you.

Number two, you have Amelia, with whom you're trying to develop a mature romance. And number three, you're in the middle of a nerve-racking divorce battle with your wife, the mother of your children.

"No wonder you couldn't handle a perfect, supple, twenty-year-old who looks like a cover girl for Cosmopolitan."

"What type of analysis is that?" I complained.

"Great analysis," he said. "Dr. Phil and Dr. Drew could not do better."

"How does that help me?"

Dr. Sid grinned. "Not you, Sam… me. Next time, hand her my card. And speaking of Amelia, you are still seeing her, right?"

"Yes," I said, perking up, "and I like her a lot. She's so stable, and she seems to actually care what happens to me."

"That's great," Dr. Sid said with genuine warmth. "You're coming along fine, Sam. See you next week."

"What about my assignment for this week?"

Dr. Sid winked. "Stay out of the spa."

On the way home in the car, my phone rang. I pulled into a convenience store parking lot and answered.

"Hey, Wise Man!" It was Johnny Redman. He always called me Wise Man, like the three wise men of the Jesus nativity story—only he called them Winken, Blinken, and Nod.

"Got your message, baby," he intoned. "I am always interested in something that will make me money. Do tell."

I briefly outlined the Veracruz resort idea, the low cost and serene atmosphere, and told him we could start by soliciting burned out lawyers. That made him laugh.

"You've hooked me, Wisey," he said. "Listen, I know a top-shelf finance guy. I'll have him run up a quick projection on a Mexican resort in Veracruz."

"I don't know," I said. "My sister does a great job on that kind of thing."

"No, no, no, Sam," he said. "You don't understand. This is Jackie Three. He's a first class Wall Street venture capital investment broker. He used to do financial projections and investment plans for big shopping centers back in New Jersey."

His voice changed. "Listen, I've got to run. I'll call you in a few days. Wisey, I am excited. It will be good to see you again after all these years. Got any hair left?"

He laughed and laughed. And click, he was gone.

13

Let every eye negotiate for itself
and trust no agent.
— *William Shakespeare*

I stood in the Macy's furniture department and watched my daughter pick out bedroom pieces for her room.

She was particular. She looked at the styles she liked and carefully compared prices, asking the saleslady specific questions.

While she worked the saleslady like a professional shopper, my thoughts ran to the phone call from Johnny Redman.

I couldn't have been happier knowing Johnny was interested in my Mexican retreat project as a serious investor, but this finance guy he'd mentioned stuck in my skin like a thorn. Jackie Three?

What serious financial consultant would have a name like that? What could Jackie Three mean? Maybe he was some sort of gambler or casino slick, or Mafia even. Was he missing two fingers, and that was why they called him Jackie Three?

"Dad, look at this," Rachel said, motioning me over. She showed me a matching bedroom suite of tasteful blond wood, complete with bed, nightstand, dresser with mirror, and chest of drawers, all traditionally styled and sturdy looking.

"This is the one you want?" I asked her.

"Yes," she said. I could see her mind was made up.

"Then that's what we'll get," I said.

"Thank you." She smiled and took my hand.

Why wasn't her mother this practical? But then practical was the last thing I'd been thinking about when I met Cindy.

The saleslady came back with the paperwork. Rachel told her exactly which pieces she wanted and asked about a delivery date and time.

Once that was decided, Rachel walked over and sat on the bed while the saleslady and I went over the bill and I got out my credit card to make the purchase.

"How old is she?" the saleslady asked as I signed.

"Thirteen," I told her.

She shook her head in admiration. "Most of them can't talk to you without bouncing around to their iPods." She handed me the receipt. "I know she'll enjoy the furniture."

"She's already enjoying it," I said.

Rachel didn't say much on the way home. She seemed preoccupied. As we turned up the street to their new house, I asked her, "Is anything wrong, Rachel?"

"Oh, no," she said. "I'm just trying to figure out how to say something to you."

"Say what to me?" I prompted, curious.

"You seem happier with Amelia than with Mom."

"What do you mean by that?" Her observation took me by surprise.

She gave me a sideways glance. "I don't know exactly. It's just that—well, I never saw Mom look at you the way Amelia did at the pool. I just feel like there's something special about Amelia."

"Rachel!" I started to interrupt, but she rolled on.

"I want you and Mom to work, more than anything in the world," she said. "But you and Mom—I don't know—just never seemed that interested in each other."

"Just a minute, Rachel." I pulled over in front of the house and put the car in park.

She turned to face me. "You two never did anything together. You'd sit in different rooms, eat at different times. We haven't done anything as a family in ages. If we went out to dinner, you two would always talk to us kids, not each other. It was weird."

"There are reasons for that, Rachel."

"I've watched you my whole life!" she said. "You didn't fight or argue in front of me, but you guys never acted like you were in love."

I stared at her for a moment in amazement. "Rachel, who better than you knows about your parents?" I said. "I thank you for letting me know how you feel about your mom and me, and about Amelia. You're only thirteen, and you know more than many professionals with counseling degrees."

"I'll be fourteen in a month," she said with a grin, "and my degree is in advising my parents."

"Happy Birthday," I said, tickling her lightly under the chin.

"Thank you." She leaned over and gave me a kiss on the cheek. "And thank you for the furniture, Dad." Her smile felt like the sun glistening on the water. "Love ya, Dad."

"Love ya, Rachel. Call me if the furniture doesn't arrive Friday."

"Okay," she said, and got out. I watched her walk up to the house. She stopped at the front door and waved, and I smiled and waved back till she went inside.

Seeing the house reminded me I needed to record the Deed of Trust I had in my briefcase. I pulled away and headed for the County Recorder's office. I had no sooner turned onto the boulevard than the phone rang and I had to pull over to answer.

"Hi, Sam, it's Amelia."

"Hi yourself," I said, beaming.

"I just wanted to keep in touch," she said.

"Yes," I said, pleased, "Me too." We chatted easily about mundane things. She told me a little about her day. I mentioned I had spent the morning at the department store with Rachel, picking out furniture.

"She is a bright girl," Amelia said.

"You know, Rachel really likes you," I said.

"I do not believe you." Amelia made a noise of dismissal. "She doesn't even know me. Besides, she would fight for her mother. She would want the two of you to be together again. It's only natural."

"I don't actually know," I said, but I tend to doubt that. "She's pretty insightful for her age. What I do know is that

Rachel wants both me and her mother to be happy."

Amelia said something, but call waiting kept cutting her voice out. "Someone's beeping in, Sam," she said. "Let's get together soon. Call me later."

"Okay, I will. Bye."

I was looking for a parking space at the County Recorder's office when the phone rang again. I sat with the engine running and answered.

"Sam!" a desperate voice cried. "It's Bill White. I'm at the house. I need you right away. Things are really wrong. You won't believe it. I can't believe it myself."

"You're not getting divorced, are you, Bill?"

"No, no," he said. "Our retirement dream home, it's turned into a catastrophic nightmare."

"Wow," I said, "that's not good."

"It's worse than not good, Sam. Wendy is lying down in a dark room with a cool cloth on her forehead. I'm afraid she might have had renal failure, or maybe a stroke."

"What's the problem?" I asked, shocked.

"The contractor is a crook!" he said, and then his voice grew hushed. "He's here now. I have to be quiet."

That scared me for them. "Are you safe? Has he done anything threatening?"

"Oh, no, we're looking at the house," he said. "But I need you to meet me here right away. You have to see the work first-hand or you won't believe it. Sam, I'm beside myself. Please help us."

What could I say to that? I got directions and sped off

toward the coast.

I pulled up to Bill and Wendy White's home site and parked in front of their house. Looking around, I saw that the lot had a large backyard on a cliff overlooking the ocean. I was filled with admiration and envy. What a gorgeous view. And the house looked great, contemporary yet an easy blend with the surrounding countryside. At first glance, I couldn't see anything wrong with it.

Bill and Wendy both were waiting for me in the driveway. Bill wore his wide hat and bandanna, and Wendy was in shorts and sunglasses with her long gray hair piled on her head in a bun.

I got out and greeted them. They seemed normal, if a little anxious. I found myself sneaking glances at Wendy to check for signs of a stroke.

Shaking my hand, Bill tilted his head toward two men standing next to a fancy pickup truck bearing the name 'Vision Construction' in a red bordering on dayglow on the side.

"The contractor's name is Willie Verano," he said softly. "Over there."

A thirtyish man wearing casual khaki pants and an open-necked dress shirt and sunglasses waited by the pickup door.

The plump older man in his fifties standing next to him appeared unaware of my arrival. He was dressed like a laborer, in light blue denim overalls and a dark green T-shirt with orange stripes. The graying hair on his big, round head was cut short, and his enormous thick glasses made him look like an Elton John cartoon character.

I figured he was a subcontractor.

Looking Bill in the eye, I said, "I'll handle this." I strode over to the younger man and put out my hand. "Mr. Verano, I'm Sam Weisman. I represent Bill and Wendy White."

The young man hesitated before putting his hand out. Next thing I knew, Bill was at my shoulder, whispering loudly, "Sam, no! Not him. He's the assistant." Without any change in facial expression, the younger man pointed to the older heavyset one.

Not missing a beat, I turned to the pudgy fellow. "Mr. Verano, I am here to represent the Whites' interests in the construction of their house."

I pointed a finger at him. "Don't go anywhere," I warned. "We are going to inspect the house. And then I want to talk to you when we're done."

"Fine with me," he said, adjusting his glasses. He pulled what looked like a Rubik's Cube out of a huge Captain Kangaroo side pocket and leaned against the truck's fender. "My son gave it to me," he said, completely absorbed in trying to solve the puzzle. "I haven't tried it yet."

"We'll show you what we've found," Bill said to me. He and Wendy guided me around the house, starting with the front door.

"Look up there," said Wendy. "The roof stops short of protecting the entrance, and there's no gutter. So if it's raining, anyone coming into the house will have to stand in the rain, plus endure the full force of the water running off the roof."

"Is this on the architectural plans?" I asked.

"No, of course not," she said.

Next we went into the garage. "See this?" Bill pointed. "The water booster pump was installed inside the garage, mounted to the wall."

"Isn't it supposed to be in a detached pump house?" I asked.

"Yes!" Bill spread his arms. "Whenever the water is turned on, the pump starts up and it shakes the entire house like an out-of-balance washing machine."

Wendy steered me into the living room and waited while I looked around. Each wall was a slightly different color, and the wall by the kitchen entrance had more than one color of paint on it.

"Well, it's interesting," I said. "A nice graphic design. So what's the problem?"

"It was supposed to be Navajo white," she said stiffly. "Not multiple shades of green on the same wall!"

"Wait till you see this," Bill said, leading me around to the hallway. "Look up there," he said, pointing. "The stairs to the second floor tilt to one side, so you have to walk up on an angle, listing to one side."

Upstairs, the door to a closet apparently hadn't fit, and the contractor had shortened the door to fit the space. It looked like a Munchkin door, or something out of a Hobbit's house in the Shire.

"It's a trapezoid," said Bill. The sides were parallel, but the top and bottom had wildly different slants. The only way this could have happened would have been if the walls weren't plumb.

Back down in the kitchen, Wendy pointed to the window over the sink. It had been installed horizontally at the counter level, instead of vertically. I had to crouch down at the sink to see into the back yard.

"Is your cook a midget?" I joked. One look at Wendy's face told me she was too upset to appreciate my comment.

Looking up, I was astonished to see a white PVC schedule-40 pipe coming down out of the ceiling and then running just under it over into the wall.

"Let's go talk to Verano," I suggested.

Back at the pickup truck, Verano was almost jumping up and down with excitement. "I solved it!" he said, beaming as he held out the cube for us to see.

It wasn't even close.

"Mr. Verano," I said, "would you come with us into the hallway a moment?"

"Sure," he said. We went inside.

"Look at this wall leading into the kitchen," I said. "What do you see?"

Verano walked over to the wall, took off his glasses, and shoved his face up against it. "Looks all right to me," he said.

I couldn't believe this. "The wall is tilting, and it weaves unevenly."

Verano shrugged. "Looks all right to me."

I couldn't believe my ears.

"Come here," I said, and led them all into the living room. "See that?" I pointed upward at the two-by-two white ceiling tiles. "The tile squares aren't all edged with the same alignment of yellow ash wood trim pieces. They're all misaligned, some with the trim to the left, some to the right."

Wendy said. "They're supposed to be one straight line leading to the fireplace wall." Her voice faltered. "It was a beautiful design, like a surfboard with a balsawood stringer in a straight line from front to back. This looks like a jigsaw puzzle, someone got all wrong."

I turned to Verano and pointed at the ceiling. "I imagine you think that looks all right, too?"

He squinted up at the ceiling. "Looks good to me."

"What?!" I couldn't contain myself. "Are you blind?"

He didn't even flinch. "Well, legally, yes," he said.

I turned to White. "You have a great case, Bill. Unfortunately, I'm not your man. With all the stress in my life right now, I'm not in a position to take on any new cases. But your case is a slam-dunk. I'll get you the number of an attorney you can trust."

It galled me to say that. But Dr. Sid and I had agreed that I wasn't fit to be practicing law right now, and he'd written a letter to that effect to send to Roxann.

To Verano I said, "I can't imagine what your bookkeeping and records look like." He ignored me. I turned to the young man standing next to him. "By the way, why are you here?"

"I'm his son," said the young man. "I drive him everywhere."

After a short discussion with Stan and Wendy in front of their 'dream house,' I sat in my car and checked my phone messages. There were two. I deleted the one from Alfonso Lechuga.

The other was Roger Chapman. He had left a time and date for the Meet and Confer at my old law office. It was to be in three days.

What was I going to do? With all the interruptions and hubbub going on, I hadn't put together a plan, made notes, or done anything at all for our Joint Settlement Conference Report for Judge Flores. My stomach churned.

Three days!

At that moment Dr. Sid's solemn voice spoke to me from the recesses of my mind: "Protect yourself like you protect your clients. Look at how you are going to behave from now on."

I took a deep breath, got into my car, and drove back to record my Deed of Trust in the Recorder's Office. I was running late. At the courthouse, I raced inside and down to the Recorder's Office, pushed through the doors, and rushed over to the counter. It was five minutes to five.

Pulling out the Deed of Trust, I tried to get a clerk's attention. It was vital that I get this recorded to secure my two hundred fifty thousand dollar loan to Cindy. Cindy had said she was going to refinance the loan to pay me back. I needed that money as soon as possible.

One of the clerks finally came over. I explained what I wanted, giving her my most charming smile. She took the Deed of Trust and went to check her records. After a moment she came back and handed it back to me.

"You have the wrong owner of record on this Deed of Trust, Mr. Weisman," she said. "The owner of the house at that address is the Vaughan Family Trust."

"She must have had the escrow agent change the name on the escrow, from Cindy Vaughan Weisman to the Vaughan Family Trust!" I said. The clerk shrugged and looked up at the clock. I thanked her and walked out in a daze.

I opened the door and sat in the car, struggling to make sense of this. What was going on? I dug out my phone and called Cindy. She answered in a voice as icy and prickly as I could imagine.

I felt like I was talking to the wicked queen from Snow White.

"Cindy, what's going on with the name change on the Deed of Trust?" I asked. "It should have both our names on it. Why did you change the owner name on the house?"

"I can't talk to you, Sam."

"Cindy, what are you doing?"

"I can't talk to you, Sam. Call Rodney."

"Cindy…" I said.

"Wight, White & Wong, you know their number," she said.

She hung up.

14

History is not to make us smarter
tomorrow but smarter forever.

—*Unknown*

Three days later, I sat in my car and looked out across the empty parking lot at my old office building.

I missed the place. It had real charm, the eucalyptus and palm trees overhanging the white stucco building with its black wrought iron railings and red tile roof. I had developed a sentimental attachment in the years I'd spent here.

Sitting there, it occurred to me that nostalgia requires recollection, and my memories of this part of my past were lost and a mixed bag. There was a part of me that wanted to walk away and forget I had ever owned a law firm.

Besides, nostalgia takes energy, and I wanted to put all of my energy into moving forward.

I had just spent the last hour in a settlement conference in my old conference room upstairs with James and Roger Chapman, negotiating the details of the report we would submit to Judge Flores the following week.

I had arrived to find that Chapman had already written up their version of the report.

"This is it," he'd said as he handed it to me.

Instead of playing good cop/bad cop, they had both played bad cop. They wanted me to sign it without argument, of course.

I opened my mouth to disagree about some of the statements in the report, but Chapman stopped me, pushing the fact that I could present my case in arbitration.

"Whatever case you think you have," he said with a scornful laugh.

I said, "There is no way I'm giving you my clients and all the assets."

"That's what you agreed to in the partnership agreement," Chapman replied in an even voice.

I wanted to stand up and shout, "No!" just to see what they would do. Instead I said, "Then insert 'division of clients and assets to be determined by the arbitrator,' and I'll sign it."

James looked disturbed, but Chapman put on his classic superior smile and regarded me with disdain. "Fine."

I wasn't going to get any further with the two of them without a referee. My best option would be in front of the arbitrator. At least there I would have a fighting chance.

He wrote in the words I had asked that he stipulate, and I signed it and left.

I started the engine and was about to put the car in gear when the phone rang. I transferred the call to my radio sound system.

"Sam Weisman," I answered, trying to sound professional.

"Wise man!" boomed the radio's nine speakers. It was

Johnny Redman. His enthusiastic college boy tone made me feel better.

"What can I do for you, Johnny?"

"Come on over to my office, Wisey," he said. "Jackie's got the financial projection done, and a whole lot more."

"I'll have to move my dinner date back," I told him. "But I can do that. I'll be there soon."

My mother had invited Amelia and me to dinner. I knew what she was up to, but there was no way to get out of it. Besides, Amelia was excited and looking forward to meeting my parents.

Johnny lived up in Newport Beach. But his office, which he rarely visited, was down here at La Jolla Cove in an exclusive upscale business park. "It's really Jackie's office," he told me on the phone.

One-story glass office suites set among giant Royal Palm trees were connected by a winding stone walkway and surrounded by beautiful tropical landscaping.

I managed to find the right suite and pulled in opposite a new black Jaguar, parked crosswise over two spaces so no one could get close enough to scratch the paint when they opened their door.

I figured the red Corvette convertible next to me was Johnny's.

The windows all had dark sunscreen tinting. I wandered along the walk and finally found the door with the name 'Jonathan Falcone III' engraved in red block letters.

In the anteroom, the lights were off. The floor was carpeted, the walls lined with standard metal office furniture. I didn't see anyone, but I heard voices and laughter down the hall.

"Hello," I called out. "Johnny?" No answer. I walked down the hallway to the lighted doorway. It was the kitchen.

There stood Johnny Redman, leaning against the counter with a beer in his hand, talking with another man.

"Wise man!" He burst into a huge grin and sauntered over with his hand outstretched.

Tall and striking, he looked almost exactly as he had as a young punk, though his bright red hair was now coiffed and expensively cut. The years had brought him some degree of polish, though it felt more slick than smooth.

He was only slightly heavier than I recalled, and his face had just a few new lines, but it was evident that success had left its mark on Johnny. Despite the brilliant smile and his obvious athletic and social ease, he seemed slightly used up and a little tired.

"After all these years, Wisey," he said with a smirk. "You look just the same! The bright little dude with all the answers!" Johnny had a powerful hand that nearly broke bones in mine. His handshake seemed just a little too firm, almost like he was intent on overwhelming me.

"And your hair's still red, Rat." I gave him my most forceful locker room grin.

He let go of my hand. "Nobody calls me Johnny the Rat anymore, Wisey." He turned to the other man. "Meet John Anthony Falcone, known both to his friends and to those who fear him as Jackie Three. Jackie, Sam Weisman, attorney at law."

Sleek and highly polished, dressed in an expensive custom-tailored suit, Falcone radiated the kind of class that comes with new money. He wore a monogrammed shirt with 'JAF III' on the cuffs and a three-hundred-dollar tie with 'Jackie III' in tasteful embroidery.

His Italian shoes must have cost easily three hundred dollars, and probably more. Something about him seemed familiar to me.

I held out my hand, braced for another crushing handshake, but Jackie Three's grip was so soft and brief as to give the impression he didn't really want to touch anyone else. Way too good looking. I knew this guy from somewhere, but couldn't place him.

"Is that your Jag in the parking lot?" I asked.

"Yeah." Jackie III brightened. "Sweet, ain't it? Cost a bundle, but who cares? Babes like it."

The voice gave him away: Rocky! This was the guy I'd nearly gotten into a fistfight with at Freshwater Frank's. I was speechless.

He recognized me at the same moment. "Hey, you were right, you know," he said amiably, as though I were family now. "What you said at the seafood restaurant? About me being stupid to defend myself?"

He pointed a finger at me. "Next time, I'm gonna hire you to represent me." He laughed. He was smooth.

"So, Wisey," Johnny said. "What made you call me after

all these years?"

"I thought of you because I had a disability insurance policy I was trying to file a claim on," I told him.

Johnny threw back his head and laughed. "I can't believe it!" He swatted Jackie on the shoulder. "This guy saved my butt years ago, on exactly that kind of deal."

To me, he said, "So you're collecting disability? Smooooth." He stretched the word out as though unrolling a long carpet.

I shook my head. "Couldn't do it. I'm still practicing law."

Johnny squinted on one side of his face. "You didn't do anything dumb, did you? Like tell them the truth?"

Jackie snickered softly. I didn't know what to say. Johnny cuffed me on the shoulder. "Forget it. Come over here to the table," he said, getting excited. "Jackie's done the numbers on your project. You gotta see the numbers."

"I'd like my sister to look these over, too," I said as Jackie opened the reports.

"Come on, Wise Man," Johnny said. "Jackie's drawn up incredible numbers here, fantastic numbers. Okay? You're gonna make more money than you have time left in your life to count. Okay?"

He gave me a disparaging look. "Look, Jackie ran his own Wall Street financial company. His father was a giant New Jersey builder—strip malls, office buildings. His grandfather was in the cement business. Every one of them a John Anthony, by the way. If Jackie does the deal, the deal gets done, and everybody's happy."

He shifted his weight to his other foot. "Besides, you need

land in Mexico, right? Jackie's your man. He's got beachfront acreage in San Felipe. How does that sound?"

What could I say? I needed investors. I'd been thinking Veracruz because of Amelia, but San Felipe might work, since he already had the land.

I looked over the investment prospectus and the financial projections. In truth, it was sort of a blur to me. All I could think was how badly I wanted to have a big project on my own, something that would show my sister, my father—and everyone else—that I could swing a big sword with the best of them.

Jackie had brought a partnership form with him. Once we signed it, his attorney would draft it into a final agreement with all the terms and conditions.

Laying it out, Jackie looked at me. "Hey, we're looking out for you, bud. We're gonna make you a millionaire."

"Every year for the last twenty-five years, at least three times a year, a client or somebody I know has told me they were going to make me a millionaire," I retorted. "It hasn't happened yet. The closest I've come has been on my own two feet, in my law practice."

"Yeah, well, *I've* never told you that," Jackie declared. "If I had, you'd be on your way to your second million."

Watching their expectant faces, I felt a tinge of nervousness about us being three equal partners. Jackie's voice still bothered me. The guy looked great—impressive, even. He'd obviously had experience and great success in business. But I kept hearing Rocky as a Mafia leg-breaker.

Johnny sensed my reluctance. “It’s only fair, Wisey,” he said. “Jackie’s bringing all the money. The three of us are going to work on it, no sweat.”

He clapped me on the back and gave me that full faced grin that had kept last place Johnny Redman on the cover of PGA Magazine and scored him media coverage in regional magazines all along the PGA tour. He lifted his beer toward Jackie.

I shook my head slowly. Johnny saw it and his tone changed. “Aw, c’mon, Wisey,” he said. “Lighten up. We’re gonna make you a millionaire.”

“I need time to think about this,” I said, folding my arms across my chest.

“Time? How much time?”

“I don’t know… five days, maybe.”

“Five? How about three?”

“We’re not talking about an insurance policy, Johnny,” I said. “This is a major business deal. I want five days.”

“Okay, we’ll write in that you have five days to reconsider before Jackie’s attorney finalizes the deal.”

“Write it in now,” I insisted.

Johnny sat down at the computer and typed in a five-day cancellation clause. Flipping the printer on, he set it to print three copies.

“Hand him the pen, Jackie,” he said.

Later that afternoon, I was driving with Amelia to dinner at my parents’ house. She looked lovely, and seemed pleased at the prospect of meeting my mother and father.

"I cannot believe mom would invite me without ever seeing me," she said, genuinely touched.

"That's how she operates," I said. "She gets you into her kitchen and then asks you every question under the sun about your life."

"I am not worried." She flashed me a confident smile.

My mother met us at the door, giving me a kiss on the cheek and reaching out to put her arm around Amelia to bring her into the house. Inside, she served us brie and dried tomatoes on French bread as an appetizer and icebreaker.

"Mmm, I love brie and dried tomatoes," Amelia said. "I cannot eat much—I hope you will forgive me—or I will not have much appetite for dinner. But it is good."

At first my father was a little stiff and formal with Amelia, until he found out she was a leasing agent.

"Oh," he said. His whole manner changed. "So you're in the real estate business? Come into the front room here. Let me show you the big development we're doing now."

Amelia seemed perfectly happy to go off with him, chatting easily about construction, sales projections, and all sorts of things.

I tried to answer my mother's questions while I watched him unroll big maps and architectural plans for his new project. My father seemed completely engaged with Amelia.

I turned back to my mother, who had asked about Amelia's family.

"She comes from a poor rural background in Veracruz,"

I said, "way down in Mexico. Her father's a farmer. He sells vegetables—sounds like at one of those roadside stands."

My mother looked first at Amelia and then back to me. "Oh," she said. "I'm impressed. She's really worked her way up, hasn't she?"

Dinner was pleasant enough. Both my parents appeared to like Amelia and were very comfortable with her. Conversation flowed easily, other than my father's occasional punch at me.

"So," my father said to Amelia, wiping his mouth with a napkin, "you think my son will ever catch on to the value of real estate? I've tried to get him interested, but he seems to have other fish to fry."

Amelia looked at me, I think to see my reaction to that little jab. "Oh, I think Sam is quite aware of the value of real estate," she said. "We have only known each other for a short time, but from what I have seen I would say he will do well with it if he decides that is a direction he wants to go in."

Amelia's diplomatic response was probably better than any reply I could have come up with, and I decided not to enter into the fray. There was no point in trying to defend myself against my father.

My mother patted Amelia's hand. "He just needs to meet the right woman," she said.

The rest of the meal went off like a charm. Afterward, when we said goodnight on the porch, my father reached out to shake Amelia's hand. "Come back anytime," he told her. "I'll take you out to the development. You can see it first-hand." She said she would try.

As Amelia made her way down the steps to the front walk, my mother leaned over to me and whispered, "She's a lovely girl, Sam. Keep her."

I whispered back, "Even though she's not Jewish?"

My mother just smiled. "Well, that really doesn't matter when you find the right person."

I had left the top down on the car, and it made for a pleasant ride home in the moonlight. I turned the radio on low. We rode listening to the music for a few minutes, and then I asked Amelia, "Did my father bend your ear too much?"

She gave an enthusiastic laugh. "Oh, no," she said. "I really like your father. He told me all about how he does business, who his partners are, and how it all works. He is very intelligent, you know, a very creative businessman."

"Oh, he's creative all right," I said. "He can create a quagmire of confusion, and then he calls me to come fix them."

"Your father is like my father," she went on. "He chooses the right people to work with him."

I just smiled, imagining her father choosing the best guy with a garden hoe.

"What a beautiful moon," she said, tilting her head back to look up at the sky.

I hadn't intended to say anything until the project had moved farther along, but I couldn't help crowing a little about my meeting earlier with Johnny Redman and Jackie Three. I wanted to impress her.

After all, my retreat for exhausted attorneys was going to

be built on her father's property. I explained to her that I had done legal work many years earlier for a well known professional golfer, and he had agreed to become an investor.

Also on board, I bragged, was Jackie Three, a rich, successful Wall Street broker and finance guy.

"That's why I was late," I explained. "We met tonight to go over the numbers and the agreement." I reached over and patted her thigh in excitement. "You're not going to believe who Jackie turned out to be."

"Who?"

"Remember our dinner at Freshwater Frank's? The guy in the fancy suit behind us who was making all the noise?"

"Yes," she nodded. "You said he was stupid because he tried to appear in court for himself instead of hiring an attorney. How is he involved?"

"That's him!" I said.

"That's who?" She sounded confused.

"Jackie Three is that guy," I said. "That's Johnny's partner, the guy bringing all the investment funds into the resort project in Mexico. Isn't that great news? Just that easy, I've got real investors lined up already!"

She looked at me a moment in silence, then turned her head away, bringing the tips of her fingers together in her lap. Clearly she was digesting it all. I waited, eager to hear her praise.

"Sam," she said finally, her tone subdued and disapproving, "I do not know this Johnny the golfer, but I remember that other man. There was something about him I did not trust. You might become very successful with your resort venture, but you need to know much more about that one."

She couldn't have startled me more if she had opened the car door at seventy miles an hour and stepped out.

"Amelia!" I exclaimed. "They're experts! What do you know?"

She looked at me. "You didn't sign anything, did you?"

"Oh, come on, Amelia!" I felt a tightness in my chest. "Don't worry. "I'm handling this responsibly. I'm going to make this project work, no matter what."

"Are you sure you're going about it the right way?"

"I'm just doing what my father does," I said sharply.

Amelia sighed. "Your father told me tonight about the pains he has taken in choosing his business partners. And he wouldn't sign an agreement with anyone he had not checked out."

"I didn't say I signed an agreement," I reminded her.

"No, you didn't. But I can read between the lines. You could well be in over your head on this deal, Sam. That man plays by his own rules, I know it."

"You don't know what you're talking about," I told her and turned away, clenching the steering wheel.

"Did you sign it?"

"Yes, but with a five-day right to cancel."

"Thank God."

We drove on down the coast in hurt silence. The view of the moon reflecting on the water only served to further depress me.

15

Try not to think of it as your money.

—Internal Revenue Service

We drove on in silence. I focused on the road while Amelia looked out across the moonlit ocean, apparently lost in thought.

The atmosphere in the car had frosted over. We hadn't spoken for a while. I didn't like that. I wanted us to be close, for everything to work out for once in my life.

But she had made me mad. Or maybe I had made myself mad; my emotions were, I reminded myself, mine to control. Maybe I had been a bit overbearing.

Out of the blue, Amelia said, "May I see the paper that you signed?"

That startled me. "No," I said, perhaps too quickly. I didn't want to jinx the deal, and I wanted to spring my success on her later with a big announcement.

She turned to me. "Sam, if we are going to be together, you must be willing to share your big decisions with me. Maybe I will see something from a different point of view. Something you might have overlooked."

That floored me. It had never occurred to me that she was thinking of us as being together, or sharing important decisions. "Amelia," I said, "I don't even know where you live! Being together? Important decisions?"

"Oh, hush," she said, patting my mouth with her fingers in a kind of mocking but affectionate maternal gesture. "You know very well we are meant for each other. Give me the papers."

What could I say? I pulled out the investment prospectus and financial projections from inside my jacket and handed them to her. She turned on the dome light and skimmed through the material while I drove on down the coast.

After a moment she folded the papers and turned to me again. "I believe you must show this to your sister Diane," she said. "Right away."

"Amelia!" I said, fighting off annoyance. "It's nine o'clock at night! She'll be home getting ready for bed!"

"Call her and see," she said, unmoved.

I looked away, searching the stars for a persuasive argument. Finally I said, "Look, the truth is that I want to surprise everyone. I want to show them I can handle a big development project on my own."

"That is fine," she said, "but show it to Diane first. If the project is all right, she will confirm your choice. If it is not good, from what you have told me about her, she will suggest a fix."

I didn't relish the idea, but how could I argue with that?

I adjusted the radio to the cell phone feature, pressed

CALL and said, "Dial Diane." Several beep-beep-beeps later, she answered the phone, her voice booming through the nine speaker system. I told her I had some numbers on a project that I'd like her to look at.

"Sure," she said. "Where are you now?"

"Coming down past Torrey Pines State Park. We just passed Carmel Valley Road. Mom had Amelia and me over for dinner."

"I'm at the Parcel Express on La Jolla Village Drive," she said, "sending out some last minute stuff I'd forgotten at the office. Why don't you swing by here and we'll get a copy made so I can take a look."

"I don't know where that is."

Amelia said, "I do. Tell her we will be there in fifteen minutes."

"Okay," I told Diane, "we'll be there in fifteen minutes." I clicked off and stared at Amelia.

"Why do you look at me that way?" She sat back and pulled her sweater around her lovely little body. "This is important."

Amelia got us to the Parcel Express with ease. Diane was waiting for us, looking smart, as usual. She greeted Amelia warmly and took the papers, and we followed her over to the owner, a friend of hers who had kept the place open late so she could make the copies she needed.

"I can't look at it now," she said as she ran the papers through the copier. "I have to get home and finish up the work on a set of financials I'm presenting in the morning."

She handed me back my originals. "But I will take this with me and look it over carefully." She gave me a brief hug. "I'll call you tomorrow."

She held out her hand to Amelia. "Amelia, it was delightful to meet you. I only hope we can meet again when there's more time. Maybe you and Sam can come over to the house some Sunday."

Later, as I drove Amelia back to her car, she said, "I had a very nice time at your parents' house. They are interesting, and your mother is so sweet."

"Yes, she is," I said, and then made a face. "And she's good at making people feel so relaxed they relinquish all their secrets."

We both laughed.

"So," she asked, "what are you doing tomorrow?"

"I have a meeting with Cindy and her divorce lawyer about dividing the property," I said.

"You will be sure to take your sister's attorney friend with you to the divorce lawyer's office?" I had made the mistake of telling her Diane's friend Andrea was going to handle my divorce.

She laid her hand on mine. "Sam," she said, in a voice that reeked of concern, "I am worried you will get upset and not think clearly."

"Come on, Amelia," I said, a little exasperated. "I've handled hundreds of divorces. It's not a problem."

The look in her eye made it clear she wasn't convinced. Giving in, I said, "Yes, yes, I'll take Andrea with me."

I dropped her off at her car and she gave me a quick kiss on the cheek. Before closing the door she said, "Call me tomorrow, Sam, afterward. Do not forget! Okay?"

"Okay, okay. I'll call you as soon as I get out of the meeting."

I drove home feeling disgruntled and a little sullen. I was not used to having someone else offering opinions about how I should conduct my business. Amelia's comment that I would get upset and not think clearly felt like an insult.

I was a litigator, for crying out loud. This was nothing compared to some of the battles I had been through in court.

As I stood next to the car staring up at the stars outside my apartment, a brilliant idea came to me. The next morning I woke clear-headed and confident in my new plan.

I started to dial up Andrea Diener when the phone lit up with an incoming call. I was going to answer, but, not wanting to lose my train of thought, I let the voicemail pick up.

"Hello, Sam," the cheery voice came on. "Alfonso Lechuga here. I had hoped to catch you. Be sure to give me a call when you have a moment. I look forward to speaking with you. So long."

Annoyed, I deleted the message.

I dialed Andrea's office and got her voicemail. "Andrea," I began, "I know you were planning to come over to the meeting at Wight, White & Wong with me this morning, but I wanted to let you know that you don't have to bother. There's been a change in plans."

No reason to tell her I'd decided to represent myself after all.

Wight, White & Wong was a good-sized law firm housed in a nondescript office building downtown. I had heard of them, but had never had any business with them. I had no idea how Cindy had found them.

As the senior partner, Rodney Wight had a corner office, of course. His snooty assistant ushered me in. The room was large, clean, and modern, with floor-to-ceiling glass windows overlooking a small park below.

Wight made no move to shake hands or acknowledge my entry in any way. He sat behind a gigantic black and chrome desk with his hands folded, his back to the windows. Cindy stood behind him.

"So, Mr. Weisman," he said in a composed and faintly superior tone. "What brings you here today?"

"You know exactly why I'm here," I said. "After I left the escrow office, Cindy had the escrow agent change the name of the owner of record on her new house. It's now held by the Vaughan Family Trust, not Cindy Vaughan Weisman. She's laid claim to two hundred fifty thousand of my hard-earned dollars, and I have no security on the loan!"

Wight inclined his head toward me slightly. "But, Mr. Weisman, we represent Ms. Vaughan in a divorce proceeding. What you complain of is a separate legal action for breach of contract. It's not part of the divorce. You will have to file a separate lawsuit."

I was livid. But the more I seethed, the more he smiled. It was subtle, but it was clear. I looked at Cindy. Her jaw was set. Her eyes blazed. I felt my insides erupting like a volcano.

"I can't believe it!" I said to her, nearly shouting. "I trusted you! We've been married for sixteen years. We have three beautiful children. How could you do this?"

She leaned forward and put her fists on the desk between us. "You know why, Sam? Because of how you treated me all those years. You criticized my housekeeping. You didn't like my taste in furniture. Nothing I did was good enough, and I was never smart enough for you."

She rolled her eyes in mocking sarcasm. "And for all those times I had to listen to you when you'd come home from the office or from court sounding like a chicken—you know, 'f-k, f-k, f-k, f-k!'" she mimicked in falsetto. "That in itself would be reason enough!"

I thought she had finished, but she had only paused to take a breath. "You never loved me. You loved showing me off. You treated me like a possession, a trophy, like one of your cars. So you're getting exactly what you deserve!"

I stood there with my mouth open. I didn't know whether she was right about the chicken thing, but I did know that I had never felt about her the way I felt about Amelia.

After a moment Wight broke the silence. "Mr. Weisman, what is it you want?"

"I want my money."

Cindy nearly flew over the desk at me. "Never!" she snarled. "Sue me!"

I had never seen her like this, never imagined her like this. In shock, I started to turn to the door.

"You're pathetic," she scorned. "You can't even stand up to me."

That did it. I hesitated only one second before turning to respond to her challenge. "You know what, Cindy?" I said. "I am going to sue you. And it's going to cost us a lot more than it's worth, in both money and emotion. You misrepresented to me that you were the owner of record. We can resolve this before a judge."

Not waiting for either of them to reply, I turned on my heel and strode out of the office. The snooty assistant didn't even look up as I passed.

Walking to my car in the gigantic concrete parking structure, I felt my phone buzz in my pocket. Thinking it might be Amelia, I pulled it out and flipped it open.

"Sam, where are you?" It was my father. "I need you right away. There may be a problem with the new development."

This was the last thing I wanted to hear.

"Sam? I'm headed to the coffee shop right now. Meet me there."

I had to think fast. "Sorry, Dad, I'm on the way to Dr. Sid's office. I have an appointment. I'll catch up with you later."

"You mean Sid the Psych?" he asked. "Haven't seen him in a while. Tell him hello for me." And click, he was gone.

I was still mad. My dad was the last person I needed to hear from now, on top of everything else. His request only reminded me of how much money Diane was making with him, while I was the one financially stressed.

No more. Never again. I was done.

16

I believe in an open mind,
but not so open that your brains
fall out.

—*Arthur Hays Sulzberger*

I sat in Dr. Sid's office stewing about my situation. It had been an unusually low-key session, so far.

Whereas in previous sessions he had been talkative and pressed me on my anxiety issues and the like, today he sat quietly in the chair opposite and made sporadic one-word announcements, like "work" or "divorce," in an attempt to keep me talking.

I had moved my appointment to the lunch hour, hoping to avoid the crowd of chattering boutique shoppers milling around the outer office where his salon merchandise and clothing would be showcased until the new shop construction could be completed.

It didn't work. I arrived to find the place filled with women.

The abundance of overly tanned, overly made up faces, expensive hair styles, and clinking jewelry made me nervous. They wore white Capri pants so tight they looked like they had been sprayed on.

And the sandals. How could anyone spend two hundred dollars on a pair of sandals?

"Sam, you're thinking too hard." Dr. Sid gazed at me from behind his desk. "That means you're either processing, which would be a good thing, or you're avoiding, which would be bad."

I started the session by reminding him about the letter for Roxann, which I'd forgotten to remind him about at the end of our last session.

"Yes, yes," he said. "A perfect example of bi-chotic, don't you think? Clinically speaking, you're suffering a mild nervous breakdown. You are mentally and emotionally unfit to do what you've just demonstrated fantastic skill at in defending your father.

"A nervous breakdown?"

"Yes. Even though you've done well for your father, you're not fully well yourself."

His face beamed. "Sometimes, by a fluke, both sides really do work against the middle. I love it!" He buzzed the receptionist on the intercom and asked her to draft the letter to Roxann.

Then he got me talking about the mess with Cindy.

With the help of his insight I had discovered, much to my amazement, that I had never really loved her, not deeply, not with the kind of love that lasts. I had simply been infatuated and impressed that such a striking beauty would want to marry me.

Now he watched me closely, his hands folded on his desk. "You've come a long way, Sam," he said.

He sat forward. "For you to stand apart from your long-time addiction to Cindy and grasp how blinded you've been to your own emotions—that is the beginning of clarity for you. And clarity is the key. Clarity brings freedom. Clarity brings hope."

I wasn't sure whether to laugh or look for somewhere to hide. "I'm not sure how clear I am about anything anymore!" I said.

"Oh, you have accomplished more than you realize," he said. "People can always handle a lot more than they believe they are capable of handling."

He cocked his head to one side. "Like the person who rescues someone from a car accident without thought for their own safety. We limit ourselves because of fear of the unknown and fear of failure. Or because we're afraid that if we succeed, we'll be expected to do it again."

His face broke into a delighted smile. "That gives me an idea for a pair of T-shirt sayings" he said, reaching for a pad and a pen and scribbled a note. "On one side, *I'm unstoppable*, and on the other, *Not now – I'm too tired*. I'll have to call Liz at the Party Shop."

Tossing the note onto his desk, he gave me a knowing look. "You've learned a big lesson with Cindy," he said. "And an expensive one."

I reared out of my lethargy and sat up. "Yes," I said, "that's right. And this time I'm not letting it go. I am going to have my day in court for breach of contract, and I am going to win. She's gone too far this time."

I rubbed my chin in amazement. "I would never have done anything like this before. I can't believe it. Look at me. I stood up for myself. To a woman. To Cindy. How long have I wanted to do that? All my life."

"Well," he said, "let's call it your first baby step."

"I'm taking other steps, too," I said. "I'm making an investment that will make my dad's eyes pop."

"Interesting," he said, sitting back and folding his arms.

"What do you mean?"

Dr. Sid eyed me with a cool, appraising stare. "Hmmm… In some ways you are breaking free, and in others you seem to be clinging to old habits."

"What does that mean?"

"Self-limitation," he said. "Another way we limit ourselves is by adhering to the expectations of others. Family members, for example. Your father has had unrealistic expectations of you since you were born."

Standing up, he rubbed his hands together. "Well, that's Ben." He smiled. "See you next week, Sam."

He held up an index finger. "Oh, and on your way out you can pick up that letter in the front office and drop it in the mail to the insurance adjuster."

Walking back to my car, I felt like I was strapped to a rocket, ready to blast off. I couldn't get over how exhilarating it was to feel free enough to fight back against Cindy.

Plus, I was on pins and needles about Jackie's financial

numbers on the Mexican resort. I couldn't wait to hear what Diane would have to say about that.

And then there was Dad. Unrealistic expectations? Well, now they would be realized.

I hadn't even had a chance to turn the key in the ignition when the phone rang. Checking caller ID, I saw that it was Alfonso. I let the voicemail pick up. He sounded as cheerful and enthusiastic as ever, looking forward to hearing from me.

This guy was unbelievable. I deleted the message.

Then the phone rang again. "Sam, it's Diane." I punched the radio's nine-speaker phone connection, ready to relish this moment. My whole body buzzed with excitement.

"Hey, Diane," I said. "Are those the sexiest financial projections you've ever seen, or what?" I could hardly contain myself. Finally, the big time.

"Saaaaammmm…"

"Well, What do you think?"

"At first glance, it looks great," she hedged, her voice resounding through the speakers. "But when you work the numbers, they don't go anywhere. There's no real substance, no plan to show how you're going to get to that impressive bottom line. Frankly, I hate to say it, but I can't see how you will make any money on this project."

The shock of her words hit me like a truck, knocking the breath out of me. I struggled to pull myself together. "Diane, what are you saying?" I managed at last.

"Sam, calm yourself so we can speak," she said gently.

"You asked me to look at these projections and that's what I see. I just don't think you should be involved with this deal. It looks like some kind of hollow shell to me, like these guys have something in mind that they're not letting you in on. Who are they, anyway?"

I sidestepped that question. She didn't need to know who they were. I had hoped for encouragement, and all I was getting was bad news, disappointment, grief.

"Diane, I can't believe we're talking about the same deal," I said. "The numbers looked great to me."

"Like I said, they looked great on the surface, but when I dug deeper I saw that it was all sand, and no bedrock."

"You're sure of this?"

"I'm sure. It's financially ungrounded. Sam, as both your sister who loves you and as your financial analyst, I strongly advise you against having anything to do with this deal."

She kept silent while I let that sink in. I wanted to argue, but maybe she was right. She probably was. She was sharp. She would know a good business deal when she saw one. Or a bad one.

"Okay, Diane, thanks," I said. And then I surprised myself by making myself more vulnerable with her than I ever had. "Maybe I have been deluding myself," I said, "thinking this would be my big business deal that I put together all on my own."

"Well, Sam, I wish it could be, for the sake of your delusion. But why do you need a big business deal? I don't understand. Who are you trying to impress? Dad? He's already impressed with you. He's always telling me what a great attorney you are."

That came as a shock. "He is?"

"Yes. He tells everybody about you and your triumphs in court."

"Really. How come he never tells me that?"

"Sam, you just don't understand how Dad works. He's never going to tell you how proud he is of you. He'd love to get you involved in one of his business deals, beyond helping him out with his legal issues. I've heard him dropping you little tips, hoping you'll pick them up and run with them."

"Is that what you do? You pick up his tips and run with them?"

"Yes. I do. But I think he makes them more obvious for me, because I'm his little girl. He makes it tougher for you. He always has. "

Wow. Here was my sister, my cold, hard, analytical sister, admitting to me that our father had always treated me unfairly. I drank in her words and felt hot tears welling up in my eyes and spilling over, running down my cheeks.

Wow, this was new. As an attorney, I had been forced to toughen up. Now my sister was making me feel like a mush pie.

"Thanks, Diane," I said finally in a voice that came out as little more than a whisper. "Thanks for understanding. And thanks for setting me right on this. I owe you one."

"It's okay, Sam. The least I can do for my favorite big brother."

"Your only brother," I reminded her.

"True," She said with a lilt in her voice. "But my favorite nonetheless."

We wound up our conversation on a positive, caring note, with no sarcasm or teasing. I hung up in a daze. I had just been killed with kindness, and it had brought out the best in me.

Could she be right about Johnny Redman and Jackie Three?

My phone rang. I glanced at the caller ID. Seeing Amelia's name brought me back to the larger reality of my day so far. No doubt she was waiting to hear how the meeting with Cindy had gone.

I picked up, trying to remember. It seemed like a long time ago.

"Hey," I said.

"Hey yourself," she answered back. "I had not heard from you, and I began to worry."

I told her how unpleasant Cindy had been, and how I had stood up to her and was planning to file a lawsuit for the money she was trying to cheat me out of by changing the owner's name on the Deed of Trust.

"Well, of course," Amelia said. "You cannot allow her to get away with this."

"Amelia, this is a really big deal for me," I said. "I couldn't have done it before, not without Dr. Sid's help."

"You know, Sam, you are right," Amelia agreed, her tone gentler now. "This is a really big deal for you. You accomplished something marvelous today! You walked into the den of the enemy and came out victorious. I am so proud of you."

"You are?"

"Yes, I am. And you should be proud of yourself."

That felt good. "So... if you're proud of me for that, you're going to be really proud of me when I tell you what else I did," I said.

"What else did you do?"

"Well... my sister Diane called. She looked over the agreement for the resort development, and she doesn't like it. She feels pretty much the same as you, that Johnny Redman and Jackie Three have something up their sleeve I shouldn't get involved with."

"Aha. And you said...?"

"She caught me totally off guard, Amelia. You saw me last night; you know how excited I was about this deal. I wanted to tell her she was crazy, jealous, whatever. But I caught myself.

I just listened, and then I said something I would never have expected to say to my sister. I told her that she might be right, and that the reason I was so excited about the deal probably had to do with looking for my father's approval."

"No! Did you?" I heard excitement in her voice.

"I did. And you know what she said?"

"No. What?"

"That my father does approve of me. And then she admitted that he's harder on me than he is on her."

"See? That was a huge admission for you to make to your sister. And she responded in kind, by making an admission that was huge for her."

"Yes. And it totally fits with what Dr. Sid said today."

"What did Dr. Sid say?"

"That my father has always had unrealistic expectations of me."

"Well… I do not think his expectations are unrealistic, Sam. I think he sees what you are capable of, and his expectations are lined up with that."

"Maybe." I mulled that over for a moment. "Maybe Dr. Sid was right on another point, though. He was saying we're all capable of a lot more than we think we are. Maybe I am capable of more than I've ever let myself imagine. You think?"

"That is exactly what I think, Sam. Why do you think I am attracted to you? I am a woman, after all." That last came out like a purr.

"Yes, so I've noticed."

"And a woman likes a man with potential."

"Hmmm…" I chuckled. "And here I thought it was just because of my manly charm."

She laughed. "That too. Your stable of horses, remember?"

Her voice turned firm. "Sam, you do not need some huge real estate deal with fancy investors to make your mark. You have already made your mark, and by following your natural instincts you will keep on making it in a way that feels good and makes sense."

"My natural instincts," I echoed, savoring the message in her words.

"Everyone else sees you as a modern-day Robin Hood…

or as a white knight. You're the only one who sees you as the unworthy knave."

"And that's why you've been interested in me."

"Yes. Without a doubt, I am a princess in search of my white knight." She paused. Then, in a voice so soft it was nearly inaudible, she said, "It has not been easy. It has taken a long, long time."

I felt an unaccustomed warmth begin to spread throughout my body.

It had been a long and terrible, wonderful day. I went to bed feeling better about myself than I had in years, and dreamt of singlehandedly defeating the cruel, calculating Sheriff of Nottingham on the way to the castle to rescue my Latina princess from the fire-breathing dragon.

17

Men occasionally stumble over the truth, but most of them pick themselves up and hurry off as if nothing ever happened.

—Sir Winston Churchill

I awoke the next morning in such a magnanimous state of mind that I didn't object when Sparky started barking. In the shower I soaped and sang, looking forward to another day of new accomplishments.

I floated into the living room and peeked out between the curtains. It was a beautiful Southern California day, with that deep blue sky, white clouds, and radiant warm sunshine.

That triggered thoughts of Verano, the blind contractor. Did he ever notice the magical colors nature had blessed us with?

I would probably never know, but the question reminded me that I must get back to Bill White to give him the number of the colleague I had decided to recommend to him.

I caught Bill on his cell. "Just out for my morning walk," he said.

I gave him Mark Hansen's number. Since he seemed to

enjoy talking while he walked, I decided to indulge my curiosity a bit. "So, Bill," I asked, "what made you select Verano as your builder?"

I could hear him breathing heavily as he continued to speed-walk. "Well," he rasped, "Willie seemed knowledgeable. He had years of experience in the home construction business. And Willie's bid was forty thousand less than any of the other four contractors I spoke to."

"Forty thousand?" I repeated, startled.

"Yes."

"And you just wanted to believe he'd do a great job. A normal human response, unfortunately."

"Well, I figured that if I could save that much up front, even if there were a few little problems to deal with after it was built, I would still save money."

"Did he tell you he was legally blind?"

"No, but I did notice his thick glasses," Bill said grimly, "and that he kept holding the contract right up against his nose to read it before we signed it."

It was going to be a slam-dunk, especially since Eric Shepherd, his new lawyer, didn't seem too interested in putting up a stout defense.

I couldn't blame him. Verano had no business building houses, for crying out loud. How had he managed to qualify for a contractor's license in the first place? He must have gone blind after he passed his contractor's exam.

I had to wonder about Bill, though. He was a really smart guy, an astrophysicist. How could he hire a blind guy to build his house?

A little after eleven, I saw the mailman pull up to the complex and walked downstairs to get my mail from him. I noticed some people over by the pool. Drawing closer, I saw Mrs. Larson sitting on a deck chair under an umbrella.

On the steps leading up to the spa, the dark angel appeared to be giving Sparky doggie obedience lessons. Her boyfriend, the big blond kid—I think she had said his name was Tommy—sat nearby.

A few other tenants passed by, and several were looking on from the second floor balcony. The mailman stood at the apartment mailbox cluster at the front gate sorting and shoving mail into each one.

The path to the mailboxes led right by the pool. I tried to hurry past, but Mrs. Larson saw me. She put a finger to her lips and beckoned to me with a theatrical hand motion to come over and watch.

The dark angel, looking spectacular in a form-fitting T-shirt and black bicycle leggings, was leaning over Sparky, who stood on the first stone step leading to the spa above. Sparky saw me and gave a loud yap, followed by yap, yap, yap!"

"Shush!" said the dark angel. She flicked one of Sparky's ears. "Shush, now!" He submitted to her command and stood at alert, facing her.

The whole complex had grown quiet. Mrs. Larson and Tommy both stood staring at the dark angel, transfixed.

"Sit, Sparky," said the dark angel. "Sit!"

The dog sat. Surprising to me.

I sat down in the chair next to Mrs. Larson.

"Roll over!" said the dark angel. Sparky lay down and rolled over.

A second or two later, the mailman came striding over to the pool area. Sparky growled at him. The postman looked at the dark angel. "Does your dog bite?"

"No," she said blithely.

The mailman turned to me. "I bet you're waiting for me to try and pet him now, so you can laugh when I get bitten. But I've seen that movie." He walked back to the mailboxes.

The dark angel looked at me with a sly grin and snapped her fingers as if to say, 'Darn, thought we had him there.'

With a start I realized the shirt she had on was a Dr. Sid T-shirt. I approached her to get a closer look. Seeing that the front was covered with a long paragraph extolling the virtues of getting things done, I touched her shoulder to get her to stand still long enough for me to read it.

The dark angel looked at me with that foxy smile of hers. "What's this? You saw something too hot to handle in the spa last night, and now you want to get a closer look?"

Intent on the shirt, I ignored her teasing. "Where did you get that T-shirt?" I asked.

"At the Party Shop," she said. "All the kids at school are wearing them."

"Ahh. Turn around, let me see the back."

She obliged. It read:

When all is said and done,
more is said than done.

I had left my cell phone in the apartment, and I checked it when I took my mail up. My father had left another message about his new real estate deal.

From the sound of his voice, I figured he hadn't even noticed I had put him off earlier. "Call me right away," the voice said. "It's important."

I deleted the message.

I was just about to go down and sit on the pool deck when the phone rang. I saw it was Rachel.

"Hello, Rachel," I said.

"Hey, Dad." She sounded kind of down.

"Things going okay with you?" I asked.

"Yeah," she said. "Just wondered when I was going to see you again."

"I know," I said. "It's been tough with all that's going on."

I heard Adam shout in the background, "When are we going to the zoo?"

"Be quiet!" Rachel told him. "I can't hear Dad." That brought a smile to my face.

"I'm really busy right now with an important business deal," I said. "But I will have you guys over again soon."

"That's great," Rachel said. "So, is Amelia going to be there, too?"

"Maybe," I said. "We'll have to wait and see."

We talked a little more about Rachel's school work, grades,

friends, what she was doing with her friends, about spending more time together, maybe a vacation or a short trip somewhere later on.

She mentioned that Ryan's allergies were not so bad now, and that he was the only one looking forward to school coming up.

Finally, Rachel told me not to take forever to have them over again. I promised I wouldn't, and we said good-bye and hung up.

The following day, I went in for my next appointment with Dr. Sid. He ushered me in with health food cookies and herbal tea, chatting merrily about this and that. He sat back in his chair, at ease with the light conversation.

"I saw a college girl at my apartment complex wearing one of our T-shirts," I reported.

He sat up. "Oh, really? That's great." He grinned. "Ye of little faith."

I had to smile. "Isn't that New Testament stuff?"

He spread his hands. "New, Old… Who cares, if it gets the job done?" Crossing his legs, he zeroed in on me. "So, how are you doing with Amelia?"

"Couldn't be better." I filled him in briefly on how I had stood up to Cindy, and told him about my conversation with Diane about the Mexican resort proposal.

Dr. Sid sat forward with interest. "This is excellent, Sam," he said, slapping me on the shoulder. "You stood up for yourself and risked being vulnerable, all in one day?"

"I did."

"I am impressed. Looks like you're moving out of dysfunctional, over toward the five percent. But you say Diane caught on that you were looking for your father's approval. Right?"

"Yes, she did. Right away."

"So my question is… what did your father ever say to you that gave you the idea he didn't approve of you?"

"He never compliments me, never says 'Job well done, son!'"

"Yeah, yeah, but there's more to it than that. If there weren't, you wouldn't need that so badly."

I reached back into my past, looking for the answer. Dr. Sid waited, and then he started talking to me in a softer voice, speaking slowly in a way that made me sink deeply into my chair… until I wasn't even seeing him any longer.

I was eight years old. My father had told me to mow the lawn, and to hurry up.

"I didn't know how to start the lawnmower," I stammered.

"Keep working through it, Sam…" Dr. Sid's reassuring voice guided me.

"He wants me to mow the lawn, but he won't tell me how to do it. 'Gas is in the red can,' he says, and goes inside. I don't know how to put gas in the mower. I just sit here paralyzed, scared to death he's going to come back out and be really angry."

"So… then what happens?"

"After a while, Diane shows up. She takes the cap off the mower, and together we put some gas into it. She shows me how she's seen Dad start the mower. After about twenty or thirty tries, we actually got the thing going."

"Go on," Dr. Sid said.

"I'm scared of the mower," I said. "I don't know what I'm doing, and I'm afraid I'll make a mistake. But I manage to get it going. It's probably the worst mow job in the history of our yard. Later, when it's all done and I'm standing in the driveway, Dad came out and puts the mower away. He stands there with his hands on his hips and looks over the yard, and he says, 'It's time for dinner.'"

Dr. Sid snapped his fingers, and I returned to me in my forties.

"That was it?"

"That was it. No comment, no explanations, no critique—just 'It's time for dinner.'"

"He wanted you to figure it out for yourself," said Dr. Sid. "Is that right?"

"I guess so," I said. "But I didn't have a clue. I didn't sleep that night. It bothered me for a long time."

I sat up abruptly. "And here's something else I now remember," I said. "At school, I remember telling some kids what had happened mowing the lawn, how scared I was. I guess I hoped for some sympathy. The class big shot, one of the most popular kids that I had always wished would be my friend, came up to me and said, 'You're a puss, Weisman. Next time, just fake it. Never let on you don't know. Always make 'em think you know what you're doing.'"

"And how did that make you feel?"

"Like a dunce," I said. "But I remember thinking that it didn't feel right. I never liked faking. Although as an attorney, I had to learn how to look like I know what I'm doing even when I don't. But somehow it always shows up, you know. The answers just seem to bubble up from my subconscious."

"Of course they do. You've got it all in you, all the resources you'll ever need. That's what makes you so successful as an attorney."

I choked. "Yeah, well, I'm not looking so successful right now, am I. I don't even have an office."

He gave me a look of understanding. "This is temporary, Sam," he said, "and you know it. You'll get your office back, with damages paid by James if you want it."

"Yeah," I agreed. "I will." I had no idea how I was going to do that, or whether it was even possible. But it sounded like the right thing to say, and I let it go.

"What I want you to focus on right now is the powerful experience you've just uncovered, Sam. You need to think about how that event from your childhood has affected the way you've lived your life ever since."

We stood up. Dr. Sid reached over to the credenza behind him and pulled out a light blue T-shirt from one of the drawers. "By the way," he said, "we sold a lot of these this month, and made a nice profit. You'll be receiving your monthly statement in the mail, along with your partnership distribution check."

He grinned from ear to ear like a smart aleck little kid and held out the T-shirt. "Here, take a free shirt. This will show you where you're at now."

I unfolded the shirt. It read:

Man is great in his intentions
and weak in carrying them out.

And on the back:

Start where you are,
use what you've got,
do what you can.

"Now, get out of here," scolded Dr. Sid. "Go call Amelia! Take her to dinner! And take her a T-shirt." He pointed to a stack of shirts on the table.

18

It takes courage to grow
and become who you really are.
—*E.E. Cummings*

The intercom sounded with a burst of '60s music, the Beatles song, my signal that Diane had arrived with our mother for a visit.

I buzzed them in and left the door open. My mother stood just inside the door and peered around, the way she always did.

"Come over here and have a seat, Mom," I said. "I'll get you some tea and a snack." I held out a chair for her at the table.

Diane was poking around my kitchen counters and opening cabinets. "What happened with Andrea?" she asked.

"I'm grateful to you for suggesting I call Andrea," I ventured, "but I've decided to represent myself."

She looked up at me with an expression of surprise. "Really? Do you think that's wise?"

"I don't know," I admitted. "I decided on impulse. And I called Andrea to let her know."

"Sam, you are one funny guy," she said, shaking her head.

"What makes you think you can represent yourself?" The way she stared at me, I had the idea she expected the answer to appear on my forehead.

"I don't know. I wondered, myself." I chuckled. "But it is working out. I've already met with Cindy and her lawyer, and I gave them something to think about. I let them know we'll settle this in court."

"Oh. Well, then maybe everything will work out for the best." Diane flicked a speck of leaf off our mother's shoulder. "One thing I've seen is that your T-shirt business with Dr. Sid is taking off. Liz at the Party Shop is real happy about that. More orders are coming in every day. Good job. Congrats."

She sounded like she meant it.

"Let me find you something to eat, Mom," I said, turning on the teakettle. I reached into the fridge for a fruit pie she had made for me and slipped a slice into the microwave to warm it up. "Pie and tea?"

I read the gratitude shining in her eyes. "Thanks for not making me eat health food," she said with a laugh.

I offered some to Diane. She rolled her eyes. "No thanks. I'll take the tea and the health food. No offense, Mom."

I sat and drank my Starbucks coffee with them.

After a moment, Mom dabbed her lips with a napkin. "Sam," she said in a serious tone. "You know I don't like to butt into your business." This, of course, meant she was about to do just that. "Amelia is a lovely girl. I think you should hang on to her."

"Okay, Mom. I plan to do just that."

"Yes, but I want to make a point here," she insisted. "Your decisions around women in the past have been a little… well, let's say…"

"Shallow?" I offered.

"Yes, I suppose you could say that," she replied, nodding. Reaching out to lay her hand on my arm, she went on. "I would have said… ungrounded. I know you pretty well, Sammy, and I have noticed how much happier you've been since you met Amelia. She is someone you can be happy with. Not like that other one. And—that's all I'm going to say."

Diane elbowed me, and I turned to see a playful twinkle in her eye. "I think she's saying, 'This one's not just after your money—or what's left of it.'

Our mother nodded. "Yes, thank you, Diane," Mom said with a smile of approval. "You have a way of saying things that makes them so much clearer."

My mother swallowed a bite of pie and asked. "Is your father still driving you crazy?"

"He leaves me about twenty messages every day," I said.

Diane chuckled. "I know how irritating all those messages can be," Diane said. "But Dad's a creative genius. If you just listen to his ideas, you can learn a lot."

"What are you getting at?" I asked, sure she was trying to tell me something. If she'd really managed to make over half a million with the old guy, I wanted whatever insight she could offer me.

"Remember when he used to hold those real estate meetings in the den when we were young?"

"Yes?"

"You never stayed in there with them. You never seemed that interested. But I would sit and listen. I was fascinated. He would have Mr. Martin and that accountant over—what was his name?"

"Marc Silver," Mother put in.

"Right, Marc Silver. Dad would sit at the end of the table with Martin and Silver, one on each side, and pour out these brilliant ideas he had, deals for this land development or that project. Then he would turn to Martin and Silver and say, 'That's what I want to do. How can I make it work?'

"Those two would hold up their hands to make Dad stop, then put their heads together and design a plan to bring his abstract business ideas down to earth. They made sure everyone would get what they wanted, that Dad was protected legally and accounting-wise, and that the project made money without too much of a financial risk for the investors."

Diane looked right at me. "That's how I learned the way Dad did business."

I shook my head. "I remember Martin and Silver being at the house," I said, "but none of this other stuff."

My mother touched my arm. "It was a long time ago," she said.

Diane looked at her watch. "Ooh, we've got to run," she said. "I have a client in an hour, and I have to take Mom home."

I gave Mom the last piece of pie to take home, kissed her goodbye and gave Diane a hug, and out they went. Once again, the apartment was stone cold silent.

The arbitration on my case with James was coming up in a few days, and I had nothing. I had been hoping to hear from Wayne, but he hadn't called. He must not have found anything fishy in his check of the office computers. Still, I ought to give him a call.

His message machine answered, saying he was out of the country and would return on Tuesday.

Desperate for an angle on this situation, I left him a message. "Wayne, call me the minute you get back," I said. "We go to arbitration Wednesday afternoon, down in the Madge Bradley Building. If you've found anything at all, I need to know before then."

With so many things on my mind I thought a drive along the coast might help relieve my tension, and maybe even spark some surprise insight.

Driving down by the ocean with the top down had a way of opening up my mind. Walking on the hard, wet sand at low tide was my favorite, especially in the winter when it looked as though the sky was about to cave in from the weight of the clouds.

I don't know what mysterious force the ocean exerts on us, but it always seemed to give me clarity. Like the moon, it exerted a strong effect on my feelings.

I drove slowly along Coast Highway, looking for somewhere to pull off and enjoy the view. Passing a shiny four-story glass and steel building I had seen a million times, I was stunned to see the words 'MesoAmerican Leasing' in crisp, giant steel letters along its top edge.

I made a U-turn and drove into the lot. This must be where Amelia worked. Maybe I would drop in and say hello. I parked in a visitor space.

All of my previous business with Amelia had been over the phone, and then she had met me at the apartment complex. Her business card said MesoAmerican Leasing, but I had figured it was a small company.

This building came as a total surprise.

The building was modern, the landscaping tasteful. Walking in through the big glass doors, I realized that MesoAmerican took up the whole building.

Inside, I approached a large, open central rotunda with a smiling receptionist. All around were glass-walled offices, all very professional and classy, with phones ringing and well-dressed people bustling around.

Shiny, expensive, and first class.

I walked up to the woman at the counter. "Excuse me, is Amelia Lopez here today?"

With a lovely smile, she said, "One moment please, let me check with her assistant." Efficient and businesslike, she called on her headset.

Then it struck me. Amelia had an assistant?

"I have a Mr…" She glanced up at me, "uh, your name, sir?"

"Weisman," I said quickly. "Sam Weisman."

"I have a Mr. Sam Weisman in the lobby for Amelia." She listened a moment, and then looked up. "Miss Lopez is out of the office at the moment, but is expected back shortly. Would you like to wait in her office?"

She had an office?

"Yes, I would," I said.

The receptionist pointed down the hallway and told me to turn right at the end. Raising one eyebrow at me, she turned back to take another call.

I walked down the hall, ever more impressed with the volume of business I could see was being done here and the energy of efficiency that permeated the atmosphere.

I turned right to find large floor-to-ceiling double wooden doors carved in some Aztec or Mayan design, with large brass handles. The lettering on the left-hand door said 'Amelia Lopez.'

Opening the door, I entered a gorgeous corner office, beautifully and tastefully decorated in Mexican and Central American art.

The assistant rose to meet me, holding out her hand. "How do you do, Mr. Weisman," she said. "I spoke to Amelia briefly, and she asked that you wait in her office."

I followed her into a large corner office with glass outer walls and a beautiful view of the ocean beyond. "She should be back very soon. Can I get you coffee, or something else?"

"Oh, no." I held up my hand. "Thank you." She smiled and closed the door.

Amelia's office had created a feeling not unlike culture shock in me. I'd had no idea! I couldn't help walking around, examining all her mementoes.

One inner wall was hung with a picture of Amelia arm in arm with Chef Rolando from the Veracruz restaurant. On a credenza stood a number of awards from the County Chamber of Commerce. On the next wall hung a framed letter thanking Amelia for a generous contribution and a picture of her with the mayor.

And then I saw the diplomas. Amelia Lopez had earned a Bachelor of Science in Hotel and Resort Management from Syracuse University, and an MBA from Carnegie-Melon.

Why had she never told me? What else didn't I know?

This I would need time to digest. Turning to the door, I walked back out to Amelia's assistant.

"I've had something unexpected come up," I said, "and I have to run. Please give my regards to Amelia, and tell her I will catch her later."

"Yes, Mr. Weisman," she said, giving me a little two-finger wave. "I'll be sure to tell her."

I drove north until I found a turnoff with no one around, somewhere I could walk out onto the rocks overlooking the ocean.

The beach was wet and rocky, and my loafers slipped on the rock more than once. I wanted to get out where the wind would blow the spray from the pounding surf up into my face, to smell the salt air and feel its giant, powerful force rising up to meet me.

I stood for a long time, gazing out across the water, reflecting. A small pod of dolphins swam past, jumping out of the waves not too far from the shore. Good omen, I mused. Amelia would have a good explanation for not telling me who she really was.

I dug out my cell phone and hit the speed dial.

She answered after the first ring. "I've been waiting for you to call," she said. She sounded happy to hear from me. "Lupe said you were here. I had a client meeting and was held up."

"Amelia," I said, aware of the amazement in my voice. "I'm… beyond words, I guess. I can't think of anything to say."

She laughed, a good, strong belly laugh. "Well, I've never heard you say that before! And you, an attorney!"

"Let's meet somewhere," I said.

Half an hour later we were sitting in the coffee shop my father loved, having coffee. Our waitress—the same one who had delivered that giant meal to my father and me before—smiled brightly when she saw me in her section. Probably expecting another big haul.

"Will the older gentleman be joining you?" she asked when she took our order.

"Not today," I said.

"Oh, I'm sorry to hear that." She laughed, sticking her order pad in her uniform pocket as she left to get our coffee.

Amelia said nothing but watched me carefully, her face open and receptive.

"You own the leasing company, don't you?" I asked, reaching for a sugar packet for my coffee.

She nodded. "Yes, I do. I built the building, too." She said it proudly, with a slight tilt of her head, but without a trace of arrogance. "But I don't own it," she went on. "One of my clients owns it. They own a number of apartment complexes, including the one you live in, and they rely on me to manage them."

So that was how she had been able to talk so easily to my father on his terms. No wonder they had hit it off so well.

"Why didn't you tell me?" I questioned.

"Why didn't you ask?" she retorted. Then she softened. "The truth is, I was attracted to you the first time we met. And like I told you, I recognized you from the newspaper article about that woman you helped, the one with the twin boys. And the more we spoke, the more I wanted to get to know you better.

"So…" she went on, twiddling her spoon in her fingers, "the reason I did not tell you that I own the leasing company and the building was that I wanted to find out who the real Sam Weisman was. I wanted to see your real face, not any attorney persona you might project if you knew I was a successful businesswoman."

"So who did you find?" I asked.

Amelia folded her hands on the table. With a wry smile, she said, "A delightful, very intelligent but sometimes silly man with a bright past and an even brighter future." She sipped her coffee, looking up at me as she did. Putting her cup down, she continued, "But one who needs to learn to verify before he trusts."

I had to laugh. She had a pretty clear and accurate perspective on me.

She held my gaze. "What you need to do, Sam, is call up that Johnny the golfer and tell him you are pulling out of his deal. Tell him you no longer want them to participate as investors. Get out of it."

That shocked me. It was the last thing I had expected. Not that I hadn't been considering doing just that, especially after what Diane had said about the deal. But I hadn't come to a decision yet.

"I read the papers again," she went on. "Your sister is right. The way they wrote up the contract, they are playing you, two against one. They can steal it all from you, legally, if they want to. And I think they want to."

She looked at me with a mixture of sadness and compassion. "You were so eager to make this deal happen that you missed that, didn't you?"

I heaved a deep sigh and stared into my coffee as if it were a cup of tea leaves. What would the oracle say? Yes… or No?

But she was right for sure about my having missed that in the agreement. If a client had brought that agreement to me, I would have given the same advice my sister and Amelia were giving me.

After a moment she said, "If you do not tell Johnny Redman to take a hike, you will never be your father's equal. If you do, it will be a positive reflection both on your character and your reputation."

I looked at her in amazement.

"You will go on looking for his approval, setting him up on the Daddy pedestal, just as you have all your life. Isn't that true, Sam?"

That thought had never crossed my mind, but now it resonated in my gut. I sat there in silence, letting her words sink in, knowing she was probably right.

Finally I looked at her and asked, "Is there anything else I should know?"

"Yes," she said with a grin. "I'd like a big, juicy cheeseburger."

19

As a rule… he who has the most information will have the greatest success in life.

—*Disraeli*

This was one case I had not been looking forward to, the arbitration with my former law firm partner.

Driving past Wight's office on my way to the office building downtown had made me wish I were going up against him today instead. For that, I was prepared.

For this? I still didn't understand why I would have signed away all the rights to my law practice. But there it was, in black and white on the agreement, stuffed begrudgingly into my briefcase.

Not a word from Wayne. I hadn't the faintest idea how I was going to defend myself.

The conference room was set up like a courtroom but without the jury box. I sat at the defense table, and across the aisle, at the prosecution table, sat James and his attorney, Roger Chapman.

I had appeared a few times before the arbitrator, a retired judge by the name of Neal Holmes, years before. He was a tall and imposing black man with a pencil-thin moustache that had turned white with the years.

I remembered him as stern but fair, sharp and prepared, always one step ahead of most attorneys who appeared before him.

Judge Holmes began with "Good morning, gentlemen" and introduced himself. "As you know," he said, "after Judge Flores received the Settlement Conference Report he ordered this case to arbitration, which brings us here today.

"Both parties have submitted their briefs with documents attached to support their cases. I have read both briefs and made my notes, so I will know exactly what you are talking about when you present your arguments."

He held up his copy of the documents, showing a large number of protruding post-it yellow sticky notes.

As a result of my conversation with Diane and her obvious disapproval of my decision to forego her friend Andrea's services and represent myself, I had given a lot of thought to my impulsive and potentially self-destructive decision.

It had not been a good move.

Unfortunately, it was too late to bring in another attorney to defend me. I was all I had. I had prepared the best I could, but I didn't have a leg to stand on.

To make things worse, I knew I was not likely to be as cold-blooded as Andrea Diener would have been. In spite of myself, I couldn't help recalling the years James and I had worked together, the fascinating and crazy cases we had consulted on, the shared frustration of having to manage some of the wacko employees who had passed through our doors over the last two years.

Andrea wouldn't have been hampered by such emotional foolishness. She would chuck me under the chin with a patronizing look and treated James as the adversary he was.

Judge Holmes had relaxed the arbitration formalities, relieving both sides of the necessity of sitting in the witness chair.

I testified from my defense seat.

The judge instructed Chapman to begin his case, and he stood and faced me like a grizzly bear licking his chops.

As he had before Judge Flores, Chapman plied me with snide questions and sarcastic comments. I concluded that this was his normal manner in court.

He probably always tried to win by condescension, intimidation, and insult, making people feel uncomfortable so they would lose their concentration, forget what they were there for, and say something adverse to their own interest.

Chapman recited the dissolution paragraph in the partnership agreement and then began his attorney performance.

He stood across from me and pointed emphatically to the partnership agreement. "Now, Mr. Weisman," he said with a hint of scorn in his voice. "Are these your initials at the bottom of page two here?"

"Yes," I said.

"And your initials are on every page of this agreement, aren't they," he continued, thumbing through the document.

"I initialed every page, I'm sure. It's normal procedure."

"Indicating that you read and understood these paragraphs before you signed the agreement?"

"Yes." What else was I going to say?

Having established my knowledge of the contents of the agreement, Chapman finished up his inquiries and then sat down in his chair looking self-satisfied. He had done a good job of questioning me. My spirits sank lower and lower.

I asked James a few questions, which he answered offhandedly, as if this were all an unnecessary exercise, just marking time until my eventual demise.

When I had exhausted my questions, I sat at my table and wondered how I was going to avoid bankruptcy.

As Sid the Psych had said, if it can go wrong, it will go wrong—and just about everything was going wrong for me now.

Judge Holmes's deep voice interrupted my nightmare. "Mr. Weisman, is there anything else?"

The awful finality in the judge's voice sparked a memory of an adage my law school professors had drummed into me: "If you don't have the facts on your side, argue the law. If you don't have the law on your side, argue the facts. And if you don't have the facts or law on your side, argue with the other attorney."

I had to try something. I was not going down without a fight. Maybe if I kept asking questions I could latch onto some issue or fact to move the case in my direction.

I held up my hand. "One moment, Your Honor," I said.

"Yes?"

"I request to cross-examine James Watkins again," I said.

"Your Honor," Chapman said, "Mr. Watkins has already been questioned and nothing of consequence was uncovered or presented. Mr. Weisman had his chance. Why belabor the issue?"

Judge Holmes turned his steely gaze on Chapman. "I'll be the judge of that, Mr. Chapman. Mr. Weisman, please proceed."

Having nothing to lose, I figured I might as well start swinging and see what happened. I got up and went over to James's table.

I stood looking down at my faithless former partner seated casually in his chair. "So, James," I began, "is this the partnership agreement you and I signed?"

James glanced at the agreement. "Yes," he said with obvious disdain.

Just then, my phone rang. I flipped it open to see who could be calling. Wayne!

I had to take this call. I turned to Judge Holmes. "Excuse me, sir, but this call may have real bearing on this case," I said. "I need to answer it."

The judge looked hard at me. He must have decided I was on the level, because he granted me a ten-minute recess.

I walked out of the room with my ears filled with the sweet sound of Wayne's voice. "Sam, didn't you get the message I left you ten days ago?"

"Message? What message?"

"I found the smoking gun."

"What? What did you find?" Thank God! Whatever it was, it was going to save my life today. I knew it.

"He changed the agreement, Sam. Are you in arbitration yet?"

"Yes. I got a ten-minute recess to answer your call. Give it to me quick, whatever it is you've found."

"What room are you in? You need me to explain this to the judge."

I told him where we were and went back into the arbitration room. "Your honor," I said, "I have new evidence in this case. In a few minutes that evidence will arrive here, in the person of Wayne Sampson, the firm's computer technician. In the meantime, I request to be allowed to resume my cross-examination of James Watkins."

"Request granted," Judge Holmes said.

I walked back over to the prosecution table to confront James. "After I left the office at our first meeting with Allen Martin, the day we drew up our agreement, did you tell him to add any additional language to the agreement?" I asked.

"I don't remember," James said. "That was two years ago." He squirmed around in his chair.

"Isn't it true, James, that you had planned from the very first to oust me and take over the law firm?"

I didn't allow him time to answer. "Isn't it true that you knew from the beginning that I was terribly stressed in my practice, that I had more cases than I could handle? And isn't it true that you came up with a selfish plan to help yourself to the reputation and the trappings of the success you so desperately wanted, success I had created before you ever came on?"

Chapman was on his feet. "Your honor, I object! Defendant is making baseless, inflammatory, prejudicial, and false accusations under the guise of cross-examining my client."

"I join in with Counsel's objection," I quipped in a moment of inspiration. It broke the tedium of the questioning.

The judge shot me a quick grin, then turned to peer at Chapman over the top of his glasses. "Overruled. James, please answer the questions."

"No!" said James. "There is no truth to any of this, other than the fact that you were worn out and looking for someone to load all your work onto."

"And James," I went on, "isn't it true that in the two years you were with me, I continued to handle a full caseload and still managed to hand you files worth over a hundred thousand dollars?"

"Yes, you did." James refused to look at me, which I took as an attempt to communicate contempt for my questions.

"And isn't it true that you continually pressured me, from the day I accepted you as a partner, to invest large sums of money in relocating from a modest, low-overhead office to an overpriced high-rise building?"

"I thought we should upgrade from that hole in the wall we were in, yes," James said. "I didn't think it presented an appropriate image to clients, and it made us a laughingstock in the eyes of our peers."

Chapman interceded. "Your honor, I demand that Sam tell the court where he's going with this line of questioning. It has nothing to do with the fact that he signed an agreement giving James the right to his caseload and his assets on dissolution of the partnership."

At that point the door burst open and Wayne stepped in. Unfamiliar with the arbitration process, he stood at the back of the room looking at me and waving a folder.

Judge Holmes shot me a questioning look. "Is this your evidence?" he asked, inclining his head in a sideways nod in Wayne's direction.

"Yes, your Honor. I have an impeachment witness who will provide clear and convincing evidence that, prior to the time of the writing of our partnership agreement, James Watkins had intended to take control and ownership of my law firm by illegal means."

"I object!" Chapman roared. "This is mere theatrics on the part of the defendant. "

Peering over his glasses at Chapman, Judge Holmes spoke with obvious annoyance. "Once again, who appointed you to be the arbitrator in this case? I will be the judge of that, Counsel."

He turned to me. "I caution you, Mr. Weisman, if this turns out to be some theatrical stunt your case will be viewed in the worst possible light."

"This is not theater, Your Honor, I assure you. Wayne Chapman called a few minutes ago to say he had unearthed new and incriminating information bearing on this case. I would appreciate just a moment to confer with him."

Judge Holmes sat back in his chair. "Very well. We will

recess for ten minutes." He looked at his watch. "The arbitration will resume at three fifteen."

Eager to see what Wayne had unearthed, I strode out into the hall with a glance back over my shoulder to see James turn to Chapman with an angry snarl.

"So… what have you got?" I asked Wayne, reaching eagerly for the folder he held out to me.

"Your salvation," he said with a grin. "But I left you a message about this on the 13th. You never got it?"

"No." Thinking back through my schedule, I realized that had been the day of my father's arbitration. The day I'd dropped the phone in the urinal! I told James, and we shared a laugh.

My spirits soared as he briefed me on the contents of the folder and its bearing on the issue at hand. I gave it back to him so that he could introduce the evidence he had unearthed and went back to my table to take another look at my original of the agreement.

The 'smoking gun' Wayne had spoken of was page three of the agreement; looking it over carefully, I spotted the meaningful detail that had escaped my attention earlier.

When the session resumed I stood facing the judge, fully confident about the direction this proceeding was going to take. Wayne sat next to me at my table.

"Your honor," I said, "Allow me to introduce impeachment witness Wayne Sampson."

The judge swore Wayne in. "Mr. Sampson," he explained, "we are doing things on an informal basis here, so you can testify from where you sit."

Turning to me, he said, "You may proceed with your examination, Mr. Weisman."

"Thank you, Your Honor. Before I begin questioning Wayne, however, I have a couple of questions for James here."

"Fire away," said Chapman.

"James, do you recall the date on which we signed our partnership agreement?"

"Yes, of course, it's right here on the agreement. June 17th."

"And do you recall where we were when we signed it?"

"Yes, we were in your office."

"And I believe you have already established that we both initialed every page of the agreement."

"Yes…"

"And what did we do with our respective copies of the signed and initialed agreement?"

"I put mine in a file in my office."

"And what did I do with mine?"

"I believe you put it in the partnership file."

"Did I put it there, or did I give it to you to put it there?"

James drew in his chin. "I don't recall."

"I asked you to put it there, and trusted that you would. But either way, it went into the partnership file. And so I did not have a copy to take home with me. Is that right?"

"You said you wouldn't need one at home," he defended. "I offered to have another printed up so we could sign it, but you said you didn't need to take one home."

"Thank you. Yes, that is exactly what I said. And after that, James, when was the next time you handled my copy in the partnership file?"

"Objection! Your Honor, the defendant is making unsubstantiated inferences that have no bearing on this case."

"Overruled."

"Why, I never touched it after that," James blustered. "What are you implying, Sam?"

Ignoring that question, I turned to the judge. "Your Honor," I began, "Wayne Sampson has been my computer repair and programming guy for many years, and he worked for me in that capacity in my partnership with the man who presents himself here today as plaintiff Watkins.

"About two weeks ago, Wayne informed me that my name was still the name listed in his files as the owner of all of the computers in the office. I acted upon that authority to ask him, on his next visit to the law firm from which I'd been so rudely ousted, to look into the office intra-net communication history for the week before James was made a partner and for thirty days afterward to determine whether there had been any emails between James Watkins and his secretary or his assistant relating to our partnership agreement during that timeframe."

Chapman was on his feet. "Objection! Defendant had no right to authorize this preposterous invasion of my client's professional privacy."

Judge Holmes shook his head. "Overruled." He turned to refocus on me. "Please continue, Mr. Weisman."

"I wish to point out to Mr. Chapman, Your Honor, that I was operating as a partner in the firm during the timeframe in question. I would have been remiss had I failed to look into the records of what happened during that period."

I turned to address my questions to the witness. "Wayne, will you please tell the court what you discovered in your investigation of the email history on the office computer."

Wayne cleared his throat and rubbed his hands together. Although inexperienced as a witness, I could tell he relished this opportunity to shine.

"Well," he began, "checking the time period you had asked about, I found the usual stuff—lots of intra-office email memos having to do with how things were going on the cases you two shared, requests to James's assistant to send out correspondence, all that kind of thing."

He turned to look at James, raising his eyebrows for emphasis. "But that wasn't all I found."

"Oh? And what else did you find?" I prompted.

"Well," he said, "I found an email from James Watkins to his assistant, Annalee Gerber, dated June 18th, instructing her to make a change in the wording on page three of the agreement."

"And do you have the memo containing that rewording?"

"I do," he said, holding up the folder he had come in with.

"And will you please read that memo aloud to the Court?"

"Yes. The memo instructs her to, and I quote," replace paragraph 15, sub b, with the following: 'In the event this partnership is unilaterally terminated by either party, all debts shall be evenly divided between the two parties to this agreement, and all assets and all clients and cases preexisting this Partnership Agreement shall remain the property of the terminating partner.'"

I did my best to keep a smirk off my face as he read, but at the end I couldn't help a whimsical glance at the judge.

Chapman was on his feet as I handed the judge Wayne's printout of the memo. "Objection. Your Honor, this is ridiculous. I submit that the defendant has conspired with his alleged 'computer guy' to concoct an entirely counterfeit document after the fact."

The judge raised his eyebrows in a question to me.

"Not at all, Your Honor," I said. "As you can see, this is a printout of an email. All emails are automatically dated, and as you can see, the date on that memo is precisely the day after James and I signed our partnership agreement."

"Your alleged 'computer guy' did a cut-and-paste job on the email before coming up with that print," James accused.

I turned to face Wayne with as solemn a look on my face as I could muster. "Wayne," I asked, "did you do that?"

Wayne shook his head—more in disbelief, I think, than as an answer to my question. "No. And I can prove that to everyone's satisfaction," he said, "if someone will give me a laptop computer. All you have to do is go into the office email for that date, and you will find the email just as it is printed out there."

I raised my eyebrows in a question to Chapman, who turned to James, who sat staring off into space.

"Your Honor, should that become necessary, I'm sure we can dig up a computer," I said. "But I don't think it will be necessary. There is another piece of evidence we haven't mentioned yet."

I turned to face my former partner. "James, I ask that you bring your mind back here so that you can look at the signed, initialed partnership agreement you hold in your hands."

James glanced down at the agreement.

"Now tell me, is this the agreement we signed?"

James shrugged. "Of course."

"Identical in every respect?"

"As far as I know, yes."

"And at the bottom of the first page, are there two sets of initials, both yours and mine?"

"Yes, of course."

"And on the second page?"

"Yes."

"And on the third page?"

"Yes, Sam, there are two sets of initials, yours and mine!"

"Look at it, James."

Picking up the agreement and turning to the third page, he froze, his skin tone turning more pale by the second.

"I didn't put those initials there, did I, James."

"Of course you did."

"No. Though it's not a bad imitation—in fact, I didn't even notice the discrepancy until Wayne showed me the email. That's when I took a closer look."

I took the agreement and handed it to the judge. "Your

honor, as you can see, the 'W' here on page three is noticeably different from the 'W' on the other pages. You don't have to be a handwriting expert to note that the angular points on the 'W' in my signature on pages one and two are missing from the 'W' on page three. See? No points. It's rounded."

The judge nodded, eyeing the differences in the sets of initials. "Yes, I see," he said, rubbing his chin with his right hand. "Hmmm..."

I turned my attention back to James, who sat staring at the wall with a vacant look in his eyes. "That's the detail you overlooked, James, that and the existence of your brazen email directing Annalee to create a new page three, with my initials in a hand I recognize as hers. That little pair of details has turned out to be your Achilles' heel."

I turned to the judge. "Your Honor, I think you see where this is going," I said.

"I do indeed," the judge responded.

"So, let me recap," I said. "James, you had been planning this from the outset. You sunk me in debt for a building I didn't want, and then you instructed your assistant to create a new page three of our agreement and put my initials on it, so that all the cards would fall in your favor on the day you called in the furniture movers as part of your plan to remove me from my office.

"You removed the original initialed page three, and substituted this new and improved version, favorable to you and against my interest. Did you do that on my copy, too, the one you put in the partnership file?"

"I would never be so dishonest—or so stupid," James said, his voice weak and dim.

"Well, and how dishonest—or stupid—would you be?" I suppressed a snicker. "Question withdrawn. Do you mean to say, James, that the agreement in the partnership file has not been modified without my authorization?"

"I didn't modify any page in either copy," he said, wiping his brow.

"You needn't embarrass yourself or your attorney any further, James," I said. "The data is in. We have the email you sent to Annalee, and we have the forged initials on this modified version of page three that you drummed up to give you all the benefits but only half the liabilities."

Chapman scowled at James, whose face suggested a man who had just swallowed a live eel. "You thought you could get away with this?" he demanded. Chapman knew he'd been had by his client.

Now I knew I had the facts, the law, and the judge on my side.

The judge cleared his throat. "Counsel and plaintiff Watkins," he said, "it is apparent from these two items of evidence—the incriminating email and the forgery of Mr. Weisman's initials on the third page of the dissolution document—that Mr. Weisman has been the victim of deceit and fraud here.

"In my judgment, it appears that you, Mr. Watkins, have committed an intentional fraud against Mr. Weisman and upon this Court. That being the case, there is really no partnership to dissolve; your clear intent to defraud means that any partnership the two of you may have entered into was null and void from the beginning.

"I now enter judgment in favor of defendant Weisman with regard to ownership of the law firm, affirming that plaintiff Watkins has no legal interest in the law firm of Mr. Weisman and that plaintiff Watkins must vacate the office premises by the end of this business day, today. That is my judgment."

I should have felt like jumping up and down at this point. It was with surprise and dismay that I realized I didn't feel like that at all.

The judge went on, reading from the agreement. "Furthermore, I see that this subparagraph states, 'The prevailing party in any dispute regarding this Partnership Agreement will be entitled to attorney's fees and court costs.'

"Based on that, it would seem that Mr. Watkins owes Mr. Weisman money. Not for attorney fees, since Mr. Weisman decided to defend himself and cannot legally bill himself for his time. But he is entitled to collect court costs and expenses."

Watkins and Chapman were at their wits' end, Watkins because he had been found out and might now risk facing criminal charges and possible State Bar disciplinary proceedings, and Chapman because he had just been forced to the realization that his client had tricked him into believing he held all the cards.

"This little incompetent deceit of yours has embarrassed me and done irreparable damage to my career," he barked at James.

"Go to hell," James countered with a sneer. "What good did you do me? I'm not paying you one penny in fees, get that clear."

"This court is dismissed," Judge Holmes pronounced, and rose to leave.

I turned to thank Wayne for having saved the day. He had to run, he said, to pick up his son after soccer practice.

After he left, I looked around the room. Here I was, fully vindicated, reinstated as owner of the law firm I had worked so many years to build. Why didn't that make me happy?

The answer came to me on a wave of insight. I was fatigued and emotionally exhausted from the practice of law, tired of defending people like James, people who didn't deserve the investment of my time and effort to come up with a defense. Tired of seeing my peers blindsided by the same kinds of situations.

I actually felt sorry for Chapman, in spite of his arrogance. He wasn't looking or sounding so proud now as he and James argued over their trashed professional relationship.

Looking over at the court clerk, who sat there minding her own business, I became conscious that I was ready for a change. I couldn't bear to spend another day in a courtroom.

The thought of getting up one more morning of my life and dressing in a suit and tie to go to court was enough to void any sense of victory I might have felt.

What did I want, really? I really did not want to practice law or be a lawyer. I wanted a different life.

Standing there looking at the pitiful picture of my former

partner fighting with his lawyer to save some small fraction of his own forfeited dignity, I realized that what I was really most tired of was the adversarial system that pitted one person against another, making cooperation next to impossible in most cases.

"James," I heard myself say, "I've got a deal for you."

He stopped arguing and looked up.

"You want the law firm? My clients? All the assets and receivables? You can have it all. It's yours. You take all the debts as well, of course; they come with the territory. Not a bad deal, I might add, given that there are so few, other than the overhead on the building."

I loved the look of puzzlement that spread over his face.

"Oh, I'm not giving it all to you for free, don't get me wrong. But I'm willing to make you a deal you can't refuse."

James sat staring at me with his mouth open, dumbfounded. As for Chapman, I could swear I saw a quirky grin playing around his mouth, but he kept it under wraps.

"Yeah, I know it sounds crazy," I said, "but I'm tired of having to work with schmucks like you. And if it's not you, it will be somebody else. So here's what I'll do: I will sell you the firm for half a mil. How's that? And that includes the hundred grand of business I gave to you when you moved into my office."

James looked at me in disbelief. "I only have two hundred thousand in my account," he said, his voice barely audible.

"What's that?" I had heard him, but the devil in me wanted him to squirm a bit more.

"I said, you know I don't have that kind of cash. I live too high. I only have two hundred thousand."

I didn't need to think about it, but for dramatic effect I watched the hands of the wall clock pace out a full minute.

"Fine," I said at last. "I'll take your two hundred thousand, and you throw in that beautiful maroon Porsche you bought last month. No, wait a minute. Make that your Porsche and your wife's Mercedes, which I know you paid cash for."

"Are you serious?" James brightened. "Because if you are, you've got yourself a deal."

"Yeah. I'm dead serious. You give me the two hundred grand and sign over the title to both cars, and the law firm is yours. I'll cover your back, bring you up to date on all my clients and their cases."

"I'll have it for you tomorrow."

I controlled my emotions enough to the point where I could feel my IQ rise sufficiently above room temperature to allow me to think, and think smart. Not unlike an alcoholic in a moment of clarity, I realized that smarter behavior was a new start in life. Happy be me.

As I exited the room I saw him turn to high-five Chapman, who turned and walked away rather than return the gesture.

Driving back to my apartment, I was inundated with a sense of satisfaction and the thrill of anticipation. Veracruz attorney retreat, here I come! I started to dial Amelia to tell her the great news. I wasn't going bankrupt after all.

Then I remembered what I had to do first.

I found a convenience store parking area and pulled off. I sat for a few moments feeling wistful. I knew what I had to do, but I also knew it was going to mean the end of my dream of the big Mexican real estate project. That thought brought me down a notch. No matter, I told myself; Amelia was right. I had to do this.

I dialed up the cell number.

"Wise Man!" The buoyant, good-natured voice of Johnny Redman. "What can I do for you, partner?"

"You know, Johnny, I've done some research and made a few phone calls."

"Yes?" He sounded a little unsure. "And what?"

"Did you know Jackie Falcone has been in prison?"

"What?" I couldn't tell whether Johnny was truly surprised or whether he was just taken aback that I would come at him like this. "What are you talking about, Sam?"

"He was associated with mafia union troubles as well," I said. "I've read the newspaper articles."

"Listen, Wisey," Johnny said, trying to reestablish his control. "That was a long time ago. Jackie's clean and honest. He's paid his dues. How else would he get a broker's license?"

"That may be," I said. "But I've changed my mind. I don't want to be involved in any business deal with the two of you. It's not good for me. We're still within the five-day cancellation period, and I'm on my way to the Post Office now to send you my written cancellation."

"No, Sam, don't do that—we can work this out, I know

we can."

"It's no use, Johnny. I am going to go it alone."

"You'll never get your big Mexican resort without us," he said. "You're throwing away millions. Don't know if I can call you Wise Man anymore, Wisey."

"You know what, Johnny—and you are a rat—you and your east coast swindling buddy can go jump in a sandtrap!"

I hung up feeling calm and confident. My hands weren't even shaking. I didn't feel the rush of exhilaration I had expected, just a calm sense of righteousness.

Someone had called while I was talking with Johnny, and I checked to see what message they had left. "Sam, this is Roxann Miller, with Gotcherbach Insurance Services Services," the voice said, "about your disability claim. Please give me a call."

I had just put the letter from Dr. Sid in the mail the previous afternoon. Could they have received it already?

I punched her up on the speed dial and caught her in the office. "What's up, Roxann? Did you get the letter from my doctor?" Have you decided to award me the disability benefits after all?

"No, Mr. Weisman, we have not received any letter," she said with a disparaging little laugh. "And as I told you, your claim has been denied. However, the company does have a business operating policy procedure we'd like to talk to you about."

Rather than belabor the point about the letter, I decided to explore what she might have in mind. "Oh? A business operating policy procedure? Sounds like surgery. I hope it's not going to be painful."

She gave an indulgent giggle. "No, Mr. Weisman, not painful at all. In fact, I think you'll find it the exact opposite of painful."

She drew in a breath before continuing. "What I mean to say is, the company has a procedure we don't implement too often, but in your case our executive management has decided to go ahead with it. They are offering to buy back your policy for two hundred and fifty thousand dollars, no strings attached. You will no longer have disability insurance policy coverage with our company."

That got my attention. "Really. They want to purchase my policy from me?" I had done a fair amount of work for insurance companies, enough to understand that they sometimes made offers like this based on the risk of future payoff on a policy.

Given that I had already filed one claim, they figured I would be likely to file another in the future. (Had they received Dr. Sid's letter, they would have known I intended to reopen this one.)

The odds were that eventually I would win, and they would end up on the losing end as compared to the cumulative value of my monthly premium payments.

"Two hundred fifty thousand," I repeated. I sat there fingering my keys, wondering if they would go for more. "That's a little low, don't you think?"

"They said two-fifty, Mr. Weisman. You know I have no authority to negotiate. My advice is, take the offer. Opportunities like this don't come around every day."

Hmm... two hundred fifty grand from the insurance company, two hundred grand from James, plus two cars that would net me probably another hundred-plus thousand... not a bad day.

And for this I was going to have to forfeit my disability insurance coverage, which cost me more than my annual medical insurance premiums? My guardian angel must have been watching out for me.

"Okay, you've got yourself a deal, Roxann. I'll sign on the dotted line of the repurchase agreement in the policy and have it in the mail to you in the morning."

"Wise choice, Mr. Weisman. Once we receive your surrender of the policy, you should have your check within a few days."

I put the car in gear and drove off to see Dr. Sid. The T-shirt buying frenzy in the reception area had calmed down quite a bit, much to my relief. I was able to go right in to my appointment.

We talked amiably for several minutes. Finally I couldn't contain myself any longer. I told him all about winning the partnership arbitration, selling the firm to James, canceling the deal with Johnny the Rat, and the call from Roxann.

He was astounded and pleased. He congratulated me heartily, even shook my hand.

Beaming, he sat back in his chair. "I'm very proud of you, Sam," he said. "Do you realize that this is the first time you have fought for yourself as hard as you fight for your clients? And the universe has responded, paying you off in spades."

"Well," I said, "Wayne made it easy for me."

"Don't understate the value of what you accomplished, Sam," he waggled a finger at me. "You have had a really big day. There is more here than meets the eye. Tell me, what made you cancel the deal with Johnny?"

"Amelia made me see that he wasn't trustworthy. My sister had told me that, but I didn't want to hear it. But when Amelia said the same thing, I had to listen. These are people who really care about me."

"And so… what's the lesson here for you?"

"To listen sooner, I guess. Pay more attention."

"Were there clues? There must have been clues."

I had to give that some thought. Yes, I realized, there had been clues. "Yeah," I said, "I should have run the other way as soon as I realized Jackie Three was the loudmouth who had set me off at Freshwater Frank's. From the moment I heard his nickname, I felt uneasy about him. He was crass. And Johnny? Fast-talking salesman selling shit to idiots. What was I thinking?"

"You tell me. What were you thinking?"

"I don't know. I guess… I just didn't want to see the clues… didn't want anything to get in the way of the opportunity."

"So how is that different from your marriage, or from your choice of law partner?"

"Huh?"

Sid rubbed his chin. "I was just wondering. Do you see any parallels here?"

"Aah." I pondered that. "Yeah. I guess I do. Cindy was gorgeous, and her voice did me in. I let that override my better judgment. I never wanted to get married, really. I just let it happen to me.

"And James?" I snickered. "I needed help, and he showed up. I didn't do my due diligence on him. And when I started to see that our relationship wasn't what I wanted, I found ways to work around it. If I'd been more conscious, I would have let him go early on."

"Okay. So what's the lesson?"

"Pay attention. Keep a check on what is in my best interest, make sure my judgment isn't clouded. And when I smell a rat, rout him out instead of giving him a nest to sleep in."

Dr. Sid smiled. "That's what you did in the arbitration, right?"

"Yes, I guess it is."

He gave me a light clap on the back. "All of this has been a very big deal for you, Sam. You have really come of age. I could not be happier with your progress."

"There's one thing more," I said. "I'm going to let Cindy off the hook for the money on the Deed of Trust I told you about."

"Really. That is two hundred fifty thousand dollars."

"Yes. But the two hundred fifty thousand I'm getting from the insurance company balances out the two hundred fifty thousand she wants from the marital property settlement. It's a wash. I'm going to let her keep the money and do as she likes with it. I'm hopeful that once she gets her fill of self-indulgence, a good share of the benefits will trickle down to our children."

"Good for you. Money in, money out, that's what positive cash flow is all about. You are in the flow, Sam. Just keep it going. That's the trick."

He got up and opened the T-shirt drawer in his credenza. "You now have a template for how to live your life," he said. "Take it and follow it from now on." He handed me a folded white T-shirt. "Here's your certificate of completion."

I unfolded the T-shirt. It read:

I survived Dr. Sid's
Psycho-Ceramics Counseling.

On the back it said:

Every relationship has a shelf life.

20

"Consciousness was upon him before he could get out of the way."

—*Kingsley Amis*

The following Sunday morning I picked up Amelia and we drove north along Coast Highway to enjoy the view and the fresh ocean air.

I wanted to take her out for brunch at a lively little café with a glass-enclosed dining room that stretched on stilts out over the ocean, capturing the full view of the crashing waves.

I had come here often in my younger and more carefree days. Of late, my practice had kept me so busy that outings like this one had become a luxury.

The way my life was going now, I felt a happy mixture of self-assuredness and excitement.

The happy combination of my success in the partnership arbitration and Dr. Sid's recognition of my restored sanity had renewed my self-confidence, and I felt good about having pulled up all my stakes even though I didn't have a clear picture of how or where I was going to land.

"It's all rather exhilarating," I said to Amelia as we drove out of town and up the coast.

Her dark hair blew in the breeze with the windows down. She was holding it back with a hand resting against her neck, a gesture I found feminine and charming.

"Is it exhilarating driving this car?" she asked, eyeing me with a flash of amusement.

I brightened. "Ah, you like my new-to-me Porsche, me love?"

"I do indeed. It smacks of adventure."

"It smacks of clean green."

"You're going to sell it?"

"You bet. The last thing I need is three cars."

"Good. Let's enjoy it now."

Amelia fell silent and turned her gaze out over the water as I drove on, lost in my own thoughts. We were rounding the curve coming into Del Mar when she turned to me and introduced a new topic of conversation.

"Since you invited me to dinner at your parents' house," she said, "I want to invite you to dinner at my parents' house."

Her invitation caught me by surprise. "What do you mean? Down in Veracruz?" I laughed. "Wow. That's a long way to go for dinner!"

"Not tonight, silly. But maybe next weekend, if you're not booked up? We can fly down. It will be a great way to celebrate your success in the arbitration."

"Good idea," I said. "I could use a vacation. And I'd love to meet your parents." To tell the truth, the thought of making conversation with a vegetable farmer and his peasant wife didn't exactly light me up, but for Amelia's sake I would brave it.

"And now you can afford one."

We rounded the long curve that signaled the approach to the café. I slowed down, but saw that the café was filled with people. "It looks crowded," I said, moving into the left lane to drive on.

"No, let's stop here," Amelia said quickly. "I want to see the view." I swerved back into the right lane and pulled the Porsche into the parking area.

"There must be something going on," I observed, looking around. "Are you sure you want to eat here?"

"Yes." She fluffed her hair and smiled. "It's a beautiful day. We can relax, turn our cell phones off, and talk about anything but business."

I parked the car. Walking toward the café entrance, I pressed the lock button on the remote control and dropped it into my pocket. We put our name on the waiting list and strolled out along a path that led to a little tree-covered area with benches, beyond the café.

A crowd of people had gathered out on the ocean overlook pavilion. The object of their interest appeared to be a man seated at an easel, painting on a large canvas.

The first thing I noticed about the painter was his Van Gogh style straw hat. As we came within speaking distance, I was stunned to recognize him as Willie Verano, the blind contractor. Willie was a painter? How could this be?

We walked around to stand in front of him. "Hello, Willie," I said. "So what's this? Have you given up on your construction business? Or is this just a hobby?"

He whirled around, brush in one hand and palette in the other, and squinted at us through his thick glasses.

"Sam?" he asked. "Is that you? Sam Weisman? I recognize your voice."

"Yes, Willie." I smiled and held out my hand. "And this is Amelia Lopez."

Willie put down his brush and palette to jump up and extend his hand… toward a nearby tree.

"Willie," I said, "over here."

"What?" He turned around and found my hand. His grip was firm as he pumped my arm up and down with enthusiasm.

"Boy, I'm happy to see you, Sam!"

I felt my face twisting into a wry smile. "That must be a miracle." I could tell that Amelia had not understood my little joke about him seeing me, but it didn't matter.

Willie went on, still shaking my hand. "I want to thank you, Sam. If it weren't for you, I'd still be building houses and getting sued." He smiled in Amelia's general direction, though not really at her.

"Hi, Amelia," he said with a little wave of his hand. "Name's Willie."

I gestured at the canvas. "So Willie, what are you painting here?"

"You can't tell? It's a realistic landscape with a sea view. Right now I'm working on the details, to give it a clean, crisp rendering."

Amelia and I stared at a red ocean curving up into a green sky. At best, Willie's painting might have passed for blurred Precisionism, though the description that came to me was more like drunken expressionist nightmare.

But then, I was a lawyer. What did I know about painting?

Amelia glanced up at me, as if uncertain what to say. I just stared at the canvas. When we didn't comment, Willie rubbed his hands together.

"You know, Sam, my son got a good job with an architect. I don't have anyone to handle my business affairs now."

"And…?" I was afraid I knew where this was leading.

"Well," he said, "would you consider handling my books, bank accounts, and business paperwork for me? I can't make out the numbers or the dates anymore."

As I searched for a gentle way to decline, a gold- and sapphire-bejeweled lady in a big hat walked up to Willie with several prosperous looking men in turtlenecks and sport coats in tow.

They pointed and commented to each other on the painting, discussing its merits as though Willie were some kind of famous artist.

I was confused.

"Excuse me, Mr. Verano," the woman said in a tone of fascination suggestive of an enthusiastic art patron. "I've heard about your work, and I wanted to ask you—we all wanted to know—where do you get the emotion to paint such wonderful abstracts?"

Willie didn't hesitate or try to correct her. Taking off his thick glasses, he looked at her and said, "It takes vision." He tapped the side of his head. "In here."

Then he turned and put his glasses back on, and pointed out over the ocean. "If you can see it, you can paint it. I paint what I see."

They listened like adoring college art students and chatted amongst themselves for a moment.

I stood stupefied. What vision? The guy was blind!

The lady said, "Well, I think they're wonderful. And I love this one especially." She pointed to a canvas leaning against the tree trunk. "How much are you asking for it?"

"That one is, let me see…" He leaned toward the painting as though he could actually see, and lowered his glasses onto his nose. "Fifteen thousand," he said. And then with a twinkle he added, "but for you, dear, thirteen five."

Not batting an eye, she dug out her checkbook and wrote him a check.

"Thank you very much," he said, handing her the painting. "See," he said, pointing to the lower corner, "I even signed it for you."

A milder version of Johnny Redman, I thought, a thief selling shit to idiots—and he didn't even know it. Oh well, everybody's gotta make a buck.

At least he was doing something he enjoyed, where it didn't matter that the angles were skewed and the colors were off. *Caveat emptor.* Maybe, just maybe, we're all thieves selling shit to idiots. Are we the thief, or are we the idiot? Or both?

Oh well....

They left, and Willie shoved the check into his overall pocket and sat down again.

"Willie," I inquired, "no receipt? No paperwork?"

He looked up at me with concern. "Why? Do I need it?"

"How many more paintings do you have?" I asked.

"Oh, I've got fourteen or fifteen of them here, plus this one I'm just finishing."

I looked at Amelia, who was trying very hard to keep a straight face.

"Willie," I said, "I'd be happy to handle your business affairs. I'll call you, and we'll get together next week."

Willie stood up again and shook my hand heartily. "That's great, Sam. That's really great. Someone I can trust!"

He looked over in Amelia's general direction and extended his hand to her left side. "It was terrific to meet you, Amelia. I hope to see you again."

"Thank you, Willie," she said. "It was interesting meeting you, too."

"By the way, Willie, how did you get here?" I asked. "And how are you getting home?"

"Oh," he laughed, "my girlfriend drives me everywhere." He called out to the tree next to us. "Honey! Cheryl!"

A beautiful, athletic, sun-bleached blonde, easily fifteen years younger, turned and waved. She appeared to be telling people in the crowd about Willie's art.

"I'll phone you, Willie," I said, and we turned and walked back toward the café. I didn't say a word. Amelia was greatly amused, I could tell.

"He is such a character," she said with a laugh.

"Yes, I know. But if people will pay that kind of money for his artwork, he definitely needs someone to watch out for his business affairs."

Amelia was still smiling. She could not get over Willie Verano, the blind contractor turned art celebrity.

They were calling my name as we walked in the door.

Seated in a booth overlooking the spot by the jetty where the seals played, I realized I had had a change of heart. "I've been thinking about what you asked me earlier," I said.

She looked up at me with questioning eyes.

"Let's have dinner with your parents. You're right, I do need a vacation."

Amelia clapped her hands together in excitement and gave me a kiss on the cheek.

"Will I have to bring my own water?" I asked.

"No," she said, her eyes aglow with satisfaction. "The beer is very good."

21

> We must walk consciously on part
> way toward our goal, and then
> leap in the dark to our success.
>
> —*Henry David Thoreau*

Before I met Amelia I would never have expected to find myself strapped into this seat, looking down on the Mexican mainland out of an aircraft window.

With her next to me, I felt a warm rush of anticipation as our flight descended into Veracruz International Airport.

The dark green landscape blended into a long curved shoreline with white-tipped waves crashing onto sandy beaches, rolling in from the glittery blue-green waters of the Gulf of Mexico. A beautiful and impressive sight.

Amelia rented us a car at the airport. As we drove through the city, an eclectic mix of modern and colonial architecture, and out into the countryside, my hopeful expectations collided with culture shock.

The people here lived in conditions unlike any I'd ever seen.

After passing through the obviously well-to-do areas, where well dressed people carried themselves with a sense of privilege, we came to long stretches of shacks made of rusty metal roofing and old billboards.

Living in San Diego, I had been to Tijuana a few times, but I had never been out into rural Mexico. It looked like the 1880s once we left the paved two-lane road.

Now we were driving on a well-kept dirt road with side roads branching off here and there. When I asked about them, Amelia informed me that they led to small villages reminiscent of old-time Western towns, with horse posts next to water troughs and cars moving alongside donkey-drawn carts.

We drove for some time on a narrow highway through rough farmland, passing primitive orchards where all the work seemed to be done behind a mule or a burro.

We saw a few tractors and some farm implements, but most of the farms were small and looked like they were worked by hand. Several times, driving around a curve, we came across cows, sheep, and goats that wandered across the road without warning.

I was impressed with the rich, earthy odor of the place. It wasn't bad, just pungent and strong. I realized I wasn't used to smelling the world around me.

I began to wonder whether making this trip had been a mistake. I wanted to keep up with my good behavior, my new self-realized self.

As Dr. Sid had put it, I had a template to follow, and I wanted very much to follow it. But I was feeling uneasy, out of my element.

I was not emotionally prepared to deal with dirt roads,

weathered old farm buildings tilting over, or the reality of chickens scratching in the yard.

The humidity was intense. I wiped the sweat off my face and turned to wrinkle my brow at Amelia.

"We are close to my father's farm now," she said.

I could tell she was eager to see the family, excited about coming home.

That gave me a pang of sweet envy. I was glad for her, but caught myself wondering what it would feel like to experience that depth of attachment to my own family.

Amelia swung the car onto a rough road that led inland from the highway, and I noticed an old wagon piled with squash, lettuce, tomatoes, onions, cabbage, and the like. It was covered with a fringed canopy, and on the side hung a sign that read, 'Verduras de Cesar.'

"Is that your father's vegetable cart?" I asked.

"Yes," she said, "but it doesn't look like he's there."

"What if somebody wants some vegetables?"

"They just throw any money they have into a glass jar on the seat."

"What if they take what they want and don't pay?"

She turned and looked at me in surprise. "If they don't pay now, they will come back later—maybe today, tomorrow, whenever—and put the money in the jar."

I couldn't imagine that.

My heart sank as we approached the farm buildings. They looked exactly like all the other little houses we had passed—antiquated, worse than an old Western movie set, but the real thing. Way beyond rustic.

She pulled up next to the farmhouse but left the car engine running. "You can wait here at the house," she said. "I have to go find my father. He's probably out in the fields. I could be a little while." I got out and watched her drive away.

I meandered around outside the old house and over to the dilapidated farm, shaking my head at the peeling paint and barren front yard. Next to the old barn, a burro stood eating something out of a broken wheelbarrow. Goats munched in a field across the road.

Well, she had said this place had belonged to her grandfather, or great grandfather, I couldn't remember which. It looked as old as dirt itself. Maybe I was right about the 1880s.

But for the absence of adobe walls and peasants in white clothes, it reminded me of the movie The Magnificent Seven. I kept waiting for Yul Brynner and Steve McQueen to ride up on horses.

I walked around some more, comforted how quiet it was around here. I could actually hear the swish-swish-swish of the big black birds flying away when I startled them. I had never heard that before.

Somewhere nearby I heard what I supposed was a donkey braying, a horrible, wheezing hee-haw noise.

Hands in my pockets, I walked around to the back of the house. To my surprise, there in an old wooden chair sat an elderly woman wearing a simple dress covered with an apron. She held a bowl in her lap in which she was separating peas from their pods.

"Hola, *señor*," she said politely.

"Hi." I didn't know what else to say. "I'm with Amelia."

She got to her feet, brushing pod pieces onto the ground. "Please come inside," she said. I followed her in through the ancient back door.

We entered what looked like a kitchen from pioneer days, complete with low ceiling rafters, a wood-burning stove, a sink with a pump handle, and a pantry of hand-built shelves. The floor covering was faded yellow patterned linoleum, probably from the 1930s.

The old woman immersed herself in preparing food at the warped counter next to the sink. I sat down at the table on an old wooden chair and watched while she worked. She hadn't said anything else.

I began to wonder who she was. It occurred to me that she must be a relative, an aunt perhaps, or a neighbor who came over to cook or to work on the farm.

She began telling me a story as she prepared the food. Her accent was strong, and I had to strain to understand everything she said, but I got the picture.

"I was born on a farm, the daughter of a farmer," she said. "My father grew vegetables to sell. We were very poor. Not much money."

Her voice was so personal and her story so endearing I was growing sadder by the moment, picturing this kindly woman in such a life.

"We had a cow and some chickens. We got by." Flapping tortillas between her hands, she continued her tale.

"When I got older," she said, "I promised myself I would not marry a farmer. I did not want to live on a farm for the rest of my life." She shrugged at the memory. "But soon I met the man who would become my husband. We fell in love."

She sighed and put down the tortillas. "So of course, I ended up married to a man who grows vegetables and sells them out of a roadside cart." She gave me a resigned smile. "And here I am."

I was starting to get misty listening to this poor woman. All I could think was that Amelia must send large amounts of money home to support her family.

The woman raised her head up then, and looked out the window. "Ah, Cesar y Amelia. Muy bien."

I heard the car stop and the motor shut off. The doors slammed. I stood up and took a deep breath.

In the door came Amelia, chattering away in excited Spanish, accompanied by an older man wearing a large sombrero and work clothes darkened with dirt and smeared with vegetable stains.

The man extended his hand to shake mine. "How do you do, señor," he said. "I am Cesar. Welcome to our home."

"Thank you," I said, shaking his hand. It was rough and powerful, no doubt from a lifetime of digging vegetables.

Another vehicle pulled up to the house. I looked out the window and was astonished to see a new Land Rover 4X4 in the drive. A well-groomed man with a black moustache, dressed in a suit, emerged and came up to the house.

I was confused.

The back door opened and the man in the suit entered, smiling broadly.

"Ah, Alfonso," Cesar said warmly.

The man came over to give Amelia a kiss on the top of her head and greet the woman at the stove.

Then he turned to me. "And you must be Sam Weisman," he said with a smile, shaking my hand. "At last we meet. I came right away when I learned you would be here. I am Alfonso Lechuga."

I shook his hand in stunned disbelief. "Yes, yes," I managed in a kind of automatic reply. Could this be the guy who'd been calling me for months? What in the world was he doing here?

Still smiling, he said, "You are a busy man, and difficult to get hold of. But I want to talk to you about what could be an important real estate project."

This was the same Alfonso, all right. I couldn't mistake that cheerful voice. But what could be so important as to follow me here, I wondered?

At that point, the woman at the stove spoke to Cesar in Spanish. He nodded and left the room. I looked at Amelia.

"My mother told him to go put on clean clothes," she translated. "We have guests."

"This is your mother?" I blurted out.

"Oh, I'm sorry." Amelia put a hand to her mouth. "I thought you had met already. Mama, this is Sam."

The mother smiled pleasantly. "I am very happy to meet you, Sam. Very happy to have you in our home." Then she went back to cooking.

"So, Sam," Alfonso said. "I am glad we finally get to meet face to face. I must apologize for never catching you at a good time."

Now I felt guilty about having repeatedly put him off. And his presence here had aroused my curiosity, about how he came to be here and about his real estate deal. "No," I said. "I should have made time to speak with you, Alfonso."

He shrugged. "We are here now."

Amelia watched us with amusement.

I said to Alfonso, "Tell me how you know my father."

"Ben?" he laughed. "We know each other from Rotary. Popular guy. Everybody likes him. He runs our annual charity drive."

Directing us to chairs around an old wooden table, Amelia set drinks out.

Alfonso went on. "I love Southern California. I spend several months a year at my home in La Jolla."

I wasn't sure I'd heard him clearly. "You have a home in La Jolla?"

He waved a hand. "Yes, a block and a half from your parents."

Amelia said quietly, "Alfonso owns a bank in Veracruz."

Now I was speechless.

Alfonso saw my surprise and laughed with delight. "You see, Sam, most Mexican banks have been bought up by huge international banking holding companies. This I could not allow for my bank. I want to keep giant international corporations out of our community economy. I want to keep this one local and in the family."

Overcome with surprise, I hesitated for a moment. "Well, we haven't really had a chance to talk, Alfonso," I managed at last. "How can I help you?"

"Ben did not tell you?"

"No." I shook my head. "He said you would explain it to me yourself."

That wasn't entirely true. My father had told me to call Alfonso, but I hadn't wanted to. But I didn't want to offend Alfonso any more than I had. I felt bad enough already.

Alfonso took on a businesslike air.

"I have a real estate development in San Diego County, you see, one hundred acres we're developing into a shopping center. That is what Ben and I are working on. We are in the planning stages, and I need a business attorney with real estate development experience to handle every aspect of the deal. Ben suggested you."

He chuckled. "And he assured me that you would not charge me for your time."

Here it comes, I thought with a sick feeling in my gut. Another huge job my father would want me to do for him without paying legal fees.

Alfonso must have noted the change on my face, but he continued with a smile. "But I can assure you, the percentage you will receive for your services will be substantial. Somewhere in the neighborhood of two million dollars. Would you consider it?"

I stood there openmouthed, barely capable of speech. All I could get out was, "Oh."

Amelia said quickly, "Of course he would."

Everyone laughed.

It took me a moment to recover my equilibrium. When I did, I swept my hand toward Amelia. "Well, it looks like my representative Amelia Lopez has just sealed the deal. Alfonso, I would be happy to accept your proposal."

"Excellent." He smiled broadly and we shook hands once more.

At that point Cesar returned to the room, dressed now in tailored khaki pants and a dress shirt that looked more suited to an affluent landowner than a poor farmer.

"So," I said to Cesar, "how are your vegetables doing?"

Cesar brightened. "Oh, you are a gardener?"

"No, no." I shook my head. "I was curious."

He began talking about autumn tomatoes and onions, and how the cabbages had given him trouble lately.

After a moment he grew more serious. "I must apologize for not being here to greet you, Sam. But it was necessary for me to speak with the foreman of our northern slope acreage. We have had trouble with caterpillars infesting the plants over there. I needed to go into the fields with him to investigate the damage."

Now I was more confused than ever. "I thought you raised vegetables!"

Cesar looked perplexed. Then in a burst of great good humor, he began laughing. "I raise coffee, Sam. A little over twenty-five thousand hectares. That's around sixty thousand of your acres. The vegetable garden is just a… " He turned to Amelia, "*mi afición*."

"Hobby," said Amelia.

"Yes," he said, "a hobby."

Amelia leaned over to me. "My father's coffee is world famous. He provides almost all the fair trade coffee to some of the largest chain markets in the world."

"You mean he's a man of wealth?"

Now Alfonso started laughing. "Oh, yes! Cesar is our largest depositor! He employs hundreds of people around here. Everyone loves Cesar."

"What about this house?" I stammered. "This tired old farm building?"

"Oh, this is the old homestead," Amelia explained. "My great grandfather's place. We only come here for sentimental reasons now and then. Did you think this was my parents' house?" She grinned. "Wait till you see the main hacienda."

Later that evening we enjoyed an absolutely wonderful Mexican dinner Veracruz style, prepared by Amelia's mother.

The conversation was lively. Eventually I brought up the resort project I had been working on, only to discover that Amelia had already approached her father and Alfonso about the idea.

"You're kidding," I said to her. "You told them?"

"Of course," Alfonso said, raising an index finger. "I like your project idea, and especially the lawyer retreat spin you put on it. Very viable."

"You do?" I said, startled.

Cesar was nodding as well. "I can easily see a resort on the lake, such as Amelia described to me, being successful. Properly handled, of course."

I couldn't put my finger on it, but there was something about him that made me think of him as a sage.

I stared at them with excitement and then turned to Amelia. Looking at me with that delightful twinkle in her eye, she raised one eyebrow slightly.

A few days later, we were walking down to the beach at Lake Catemaco carrying towels, chairs, and a beer cooler. I still could not believe all that had happened, or how quickly it had fallen into place.

Alfonso had agreed to finance the retreat project, based of course, at Amelia's insistence, on a financial plan drawn up by my sister. Cesar was happy to lease us the land bordering the lake.

Amelia had spoken to Chef Rolando. He would be coming down to set up the kitchen, and would hire local staff he knew and trusted.

I had talked several times to Dr. Sid and finally persuaded him to come down and be the keynote speaker at the opening ceremony.

The marketing campaign design was nearly completed, and soon we would be preparing for the grand opening. The plan was to bring attorneys down for retreats, and while they were here we would acquaint them with the many benefits of ground-floor membership in the retreat.

Word of mouth was spreading already. I was nothing if not excited.

The best things in life are free- But you can keep them for the birds and bees- Now give me money (that what I want) blasted out of the cell phone in my pocket. I hadn't talked to my father in a while. I gestured to Amelia, put down our things, and opened the phone. "How are you, Dad?"

"Sam!" He bulled right to the point. "I have a really big problem with my new development. They served me with a lawsuit, can you believe that? I need you to come back to the states tomorrow to straighten them out."

He sounded really agitated.

Calmly I said, "Just a second, Dad. I have to go get a beer." Amelia frowned, obviously concerned about what I was doing. I held up a finger for her to hold on a moment. She seemed unsure, but watched me.

I opened a beer from the cooler and drank it half down, and waited another minute before picking up the phone again.

As if no time had passed, I said cheerily, "Okay, Dad, what was that again?"

I heard a hearty chuckle on other end of the line. My father said, "Congratulations, son. I know you're going to succeed with your project. I'll have my company attorney handle this thing up here. Tell Amelia hello for me." And he hung up.

I looked at Amelia. "He has never talked like that to me before, never in my life."

"How is that?" she asked.

I picked up our stuff and kept walking. As we approached

the lakeside, I said, "My father has never acknowledged my achievement like that. He actually said 'Congratulations.' That's an absolute first. First time ever."

"You have learned the right way to handle things, and he is proud."

We walked a little further, and I had a moment of clarity. "You know, you could be right," I said. "Diane tried to tell me. Dad has been doing this to teach me. And he just kept doing it until I got it."

I had finally learned to say 'no,' even to my father. It had only taken me fifty years. Good thing I wasn't a woman, or I would have been pregnant every week. I wondered what I would learn in the next fifty years.

A little later, Amelia and I sat by ourselves in our lounge chairs on the beach of Lake Catemaco, drinking and chatting in the velvet twilight under the starkly beautiful Mexican moon. The air was warm, moist, and heavy with lush tropical scents.

My father's phone call still preoccupied me. It marked such a change for me that I couldn't get it out of my mind.

I had finally learned the lesson he had been trying to teach me for so many years, a lesson he'd known all along I would eventually catch on to. And he had kept at me until I did.

I smiled and raised my beer bottle. "To my father," I said to Amelia.

"To both our fathers," she said, raising her bottle.

We drank in warm contentment, gazing out at the magnificent lake.

"I really want to bring the kids down here when it's finished," I said.

"Oh, would you do that?" she asked eagerly. "I think we would all have great fun." As though she had just thought of something awful, her face clouded. "Do you still miss your wife?"

"Are you kidding?" I snorted. My marriage is a closed chapter in my life." I grinned inwardly. "Though maybe it's not entirely closed from her point of view."

I glanced sidelong at Amelia to see how she would take that. Sure enough, her brow furrowed with concern. I let her ruminate for a minute, just for the heck of it, before giving her the punch line. "Her feelings for me are so strong that she told me that if I were to die, she would go to my funeral just to make sure I was really dead."

Amelia edged a playful elbow into my ribs. "Oh, you are so mean!" she declared, but her eyes were dancing now.

I gestured at her with my bottle. "By the way, where'd you get that pink T-shirt?" The slogan on it read:

The attitude you send out
is the attitude you get back.

The quote was attributed in finer print to one William Ury.

"Neiman Marcus," she said.

I nodded my appreciation. "Looks good on you." Only mildly suggestive, it clung nicely to her body.

I smiled to myself and looked around us. Dozens of truckloads of sand had been brought in to make this new beach area.

Big heavy yellow earthmoving equipment was parked all around. Survey cones, yellow safety tape, and bright orange surveyor's string and posts were laid out where the retreat was being built.

I was overcome with a profound joy and excitement that took me back to the feeling I'd known in my twenties and thirties. It was all really happening, my big project. I had done it.

Dr. Sid had been right. I was creating my own happiness, just as I had created my own problems, and I could solve any problem I could create. I hoped I wouldn't find it necessary in the future to test myself on that.

I watched as some exotic jungle bird flew out over the water. "Don't you think it's awfully coincidental," I said, "that you showed up in my life, along with Alfonso, who knows my father and everyone here too?"

She wrinkled her brow in thought. "What made you call MesoAmerican Leasing in the first place?" she asked, tilting her head at me with a gleam in her eye.

I had to think a second. Then suddenly it was all clear. "You're going to love this," I grinned. "I found your card stuck in the visor of my car when Cindy threw me out of the house. That was how I decided to call you in the first place."

"How did my card get stuck in your visor?" she asked.

"I think my father gave it to me." I sat back and let loose

with a full belly laugh. "Alfonso must have given it to him in case he ever wanted a leasing agent—you know, to boost your business. And then Dad gave it to me, not even thinking of anything in particular, just in the event I ever needed a leasing agent."

She smiled sweetly. "And so you called."

"And so I called," I said, squeezing her hand. But then I realized I had a question of my own. "So why did the card say 'agent,' and not 'broker'?"

"I never did like the word 'broker,'" she said. " I went into business to make a profit, not to go broke. Or broker." She laughed. "No way!"

"I see the logic in that." It all felt so good and so right. This was such a strange feeling, being happy.

I looked over at Amelia. "There's no sign here."

"What?"

I stood up. Not hesitating a second, I tore off my T-shirt, pulled down my swim trunks, and walked proudly into the lake. The water was cool and smelled like tropical jungle, but I didn't care. It felt wonderful.

Giggling, Amelia jumped up and pulled off her clothes. She came running into the water after me, laughing and splashing.

The End … for now

About the Author

A retired attorney, Robert Gottlieb maintained a private practice in Los Angeles and San Diego for a total of 35 years. He began his general law practice focusing primarily on business clients, and in the 1980s began representing insurance company clients. His career as a lawyer provides the backdrop of experience against which he has painted with a broad stroke the disillusionment and exhaustion that haunt the majority of attorneys practicing today.

Born in Los Angeles, Robert lived most of his early life in the San Fernando Valley. He attended public school and graduated from law school in Los Angeles.

Realizing that Los Angeles was a magnet for the world of dreamers seeking recognition and success in the arts and entertainment field, Robert conjured a theory that God created earthquakes for the purpose of bringing talent and the crazies to Hollywood, shaking the world until the fallout from other countries ended up in the United States.

God then shook the world again, according to the theory, and whatever had originally fallen into the United States now fell into California. God shook the world with yet another earth quake, and what shook loose fell into Hollywood, bringing ideas ranging from the bizarre to the ingenious and elevating a few to enjoyment of huge success.

Early in his days as a practicing attorney, Robert began making and saving notes involving situations with clients, prospective clients, courtroom proceedings, and the humorous and often absurd stories related to him by other attorneys. It didn't take long to realize that the practice of law, like any other business, is about people much more than about the law itself.

In the mid- to late 1990s, Robert began to create narratives from his notes. *IQ Room Temperature* is his first novel.